AGAINST THE WIND

WAYWARD SONS
BOOK 3

HARPER JACKSON

ONE

GABI

Nina Lambert, the office manager and general keeper of all records for Island Medical, threw the lock on the front door of the clinic. "Survived another one."

I fought the urge to wilt into the nearest chair. If I did, chances were I wouldn't be getting up again anytime soon. "Couldn't have done it without you. Why did no one tell me what a terrible idea it would be for me to run the clinic on my own with Dr. Sibley on vacation? If I didn't know better, I'd say this was his version of hazing the newbie."

I'd been back on Hatterwick for just a month and a half since I'd completed my residency down in New Orleans. I'd harbored delusions that the pace of my small hometown of Sutter's Ferry would be slower. In reality, I felt as if I'd hit the ground at a dead sprint and hadn't stopped yet.

Kristie Turner, one of our nurses, scraped the hair back from her face and redid her messy bun. "To be fair, I don't think Doc *deliberately* planned his vacation for when a hurricane was gonna hit the island."

"Well, even if he had, not like he could get back from Cancun in time to help."

For a few days, we'd thought the storm might skew out to sea, but weather reports from this afternoon quashed that possibility. The hurricane warning had been issued, and everyone on the island was behaving accordingly. Which meant we'd had a spate of injuries and accidents around hurricane prep, in addition to the usual fare of summer colds, swimmer's ear, and sprains. It also meant that my team of nurses and I were the only official medical professionals on the island, other than the EMTs and paramedics with the fire department. I'd have been lying if I didn't admit that prospect was intimidating as hell.

I scooped a hand through my hair. "Let's get out of here, y'all. I suspect tomorrow's gonna be even worse."

We rushed through the end-of-day close-up routine. I waved my staff on out, while I made a few last-minute chart notes about some of today's patients. I found them easier to do in the quiet, and I needed a little time to file the rough edges off my day before I headed home to my sister's house. I was staying with her and her family until I found a place of my own—something I hadn't expected to take quite this long. But with my full attention going to getting settled in at the clinic, there'd been no time. Not to mention everything else going on in the past month.

By the time I locked the back door of the clinic and walked out to my car, it was getting on toward suppertime. Caroline would have something ready, but much as I adored her and the rest of the family, I wasn't yet up for dealing with the enthusiasm of my niece and nephew. Sliding behind the wheel, I made the snap decision to stop by OBX Brewhouse for a drink before I headed home. Caroline's husband, Hoyt, was a firefighter, so the rule of the house was that you ate when you could. Dinner would be there whenever I made it home.

The two-story wood building housing OBX Brewhouse stood open for business as usual, with the awning windows propped open to take advantage of the cross breezes. Quite a few patrons nursed pints of custom brews in rocking chairs on the wraparound porch or scattered at various outdoor tables. The industrial-meets-beach aesthetic had been all Bree's vision when she and her grandfather, Ed, rebuilt after a fire destroyed the original building that dated back to the 1920s, when it had been used to process fish coming in off the docks. Now gleaming copper brewing tanks stretched up two stories behind walls of reclaimed windows hung to create a division of the space without blocking the view of the process going on beyond. Reclaimed heart pine floors spread throughout the taproom, and big industrial fans above made lazy circles, stirring the faintly salty air.

The mingled aromas of beer, fried fish, and wood polish tickled my nose as I paused in the entryway. The dinner crowd filled maybe half the tables inside—mostly locals taking advantage of the calm before the storm slated to hit day after tomorrow. A cover of "Southern Cross" drifted from the sound system, not quite drowning out the rhythm of conversation and clinking glasses. Bree stood behind the bar, her blonde hair pulled back in a messy knot as she filled a flight of taster glasses. She looked up as I stepped up to the bar, a smile tipping up one corner of the mouth perpetually set in a sarcastic smirk.

"If it isn't my favorite doctor." She slid the flight across to a couple I didn't recognize—tourists who either hadn't gotten the memo about the incoming hurricane or didn't care—and made her way over to my end of the bar. The polished wood surface gleamed under the warm Edison bulb lighting, and I could hear the subtle hiss of carbonation from the taps behind her. "You look like you need a drink."

"That obvious?" I settled onto one of the worn leather bar

stools, letting my shoulders finally drop from where they'd been hunched up around my ears for most of the day.

"Only to someone who's known you since middle school." She reached for a glass from the rack overhead. The familiar ritual was oddly comforting after the chaos of the clinic. "The usual?"

I nodded, claiming the spot and letting the ambient noise of the brewhouse wash over me. The usual was the house IPA, which I'd helped Bree test and refine during a visit home back when she'd first started brewing. It had taken us three tries to get the hops balance just right, but the result was perfection—crisp and citrusy with just enough bite to cut through the humid coastal air. "Your grandfather's not in tonight?"

"Nah, he's battening down the hatches at home. Though knowing Pop, he'll show up tomorrow anyway, storm or no storm." She set the beer in front of me, the glass frosted and perfect, a thin head of foam crowning the golden liquid. The condensation immediately began beading on the outside in the humid air. "You eaten?"

I wrapped my fingers around the cool glass, savoring the contrast against my warm palms. "Not yet. But Caroline will have food at the house when I get back. I just needed a little more decompression first. It was a hell of a day at the clinic."

"Storm shit?" Bree asked, already knowing the answer as she wiped down the bar.

"Of course. Last-minute checkups, prescription refills, people panicking about whether they have enough insulin or blood pressure meds to ride out a potential evacuation." I took a long pull of the IPA, feeling some of the day's tension start to unknot in my shoulders. "Y'all ready for what's coming?"

"There will be some prep still to do around here tomorrow morning. Boarding up the big windows, securing the outdoor furniture, making sure the generators are topped off." She gestured toward the wall of reclaimed windows that separated the taproom from the brewing area. "But we've been through this dance before. You ready for your first hurricane back on the island as the only medical professional?"

I sipped my beer, considering the weight of that responsibility. "Ready might be a strong word. But I'm here, and I signed up for this when I decided to come back. The only doctor on-island, so far as I know."

Bree's eyebrows shot up toward her hairline. "Only? What about Dr. Sibley?"

"He's on vacation in Mexico with his wife. Twentieth wedding anniversary, apparently." I couldn't keep the slight edge of frustration out of my voice. "Booked it months ago, long before anyone knew we'd have a Category 3 bearing down on us."

"Shit timing on his part. But I have faith you're up to the task. You always were the smartest one in your class."

"Glad somebody thinks so." I traced a finger through the condensation on my glass, watching the droplets reform.

She swiped at a wet spot on the bar with her towel, then looked up with the kind of casual expression that usually meant she was fishing for information. "Hey, have you heard from Willa lately?"

Willa Sutter, one of my oldest friends and Bree's former roommate, had just eloped last week with her lifelong crush, Sawyer Malone. Prior to news of the hurricane, their spontaneous wedding had been the talk of the town gossip chain, with everyone from the grocery store checkout ladies to the guys at the marina weighing in on the romance of it all.

"She popped in a couple of days after the wedding to get a prescription refilled." I smiled, remembering how absolutely radiant she'd looked, practically glowing with happiness. That spontaneous elopement meant she hadn't gotten around to birth control before the wedding, but I'd handled that discreetly. "But not since then. I think she's trying to live her best newlywed life, holed up at Sutter House."

"God knows, she deserves it after everything she's been through." Bree's expression softened with genuine affection.

Willa was the poster girl proof that coming from money and privilege didn't mean she had a good family. She'd been estranged from her parents since she'd turned eighteen, and while she'd never talked openly about the specifics, the emotional scars were easy enough to see if you knew what to look for.

"Gotta be weird for you not having her at home anymore. Y'all roomed together for several years, right?" I asked, genuinely curious about how the transition was going.

"Yeah, ever since she moved back to the island full-time. It's stupid quiet at the cottage now. I even miss that big lug of a dog following me around, begging for scraps."

Willa's pit bull, Roy Kent—named after the character *Ted Lasso*—was her well-known shadow. She seldom went anywhere without him, which I knew was as much because she genuinely loved dogs as because of her social anxiety. The massive black dog was something of a town mascot.

"Did you see this coming? Her and Sawyer, I mean." Since I'd been away for medical school and residency, missing years of the subtle social dynamics, I wanted Bree's perspective on the romance that had apparently been brewing under everyone's noses.

"Oh, I've suspected they had a thing for each other for years. The way they look at each other when they think nobody's watching, the way he always finds excuses to check on her." Bree smiled, but there was something wistful in it. "I confess, I didn't quite expect it to go down the way it did, but so long as she's happy, that's what matters to me."

"No question about that. Sawyer's been such a big support, helping her out with her grandfather's funeral arrangements and facing down her parents when they tried to interfere." Part of me wondered how much all of those traumatic events had pushed them to take the leap and tie the knot so they could be their own family, their own support system. I sighed, thinking of all the ways he'd stepped up to protect Willa when she needed it most. "It's nice to know at least some people have better luck in love."

It was more than I meant to say, the words slipping out on a tide of beer and exhaustion.

Bree's gaze sharpened at the bitter undertone. "There a story behind that comment?"

I took another long sip, buying myself time to decide how much I wanted to share. "Not one worth telling, really. I was involved with this guy back in New Orleans. Thought it was serious, thought we were building toward something real." The memory still stung, even weeks later. "Turned out it was more of a situationship than a real relationship. More fool me."

I washed down the bitter taste in my mouth with more of the excellent IPA, not wanting to dwell on the shadow that had cast a pall over the last weeks of my residency.

"What's going on in your love life?" I asked, deflecting the attention back to her. "Anyone interesting on your radar?"

Bree scoffed, the sound sharp in the ambient noise of the brewhouse. "What love life? Between running this place and keeping tabs on Pop to make sure he doesn't overdo it, I don't have time for anything other than the occasional casual hookup."

I wasn't a hundred percent sure that was the whole truth. Even as busy as Bree was running the Brewhouse and managing her grandfather's stubborn independence, if there was someone truly worth it, I thought she'd make the time. But

I also knew she had old wounds that ran deep—everyone on the island knew about the falling out with Ford Donoghue years ago, even if the details remained frustratingly vague.

Way back before I'd left for college, Caroline and I had thought for a bit that Bree was finally going to get together with her long-term best friend, Ford Donoghue. Ford was also best friends with our brother, Rios; Willa's husband, Sawyer; and Willa's elder brother, Jace. They'd been thick as thieves from elementary school on. The Wayward Sons, they'd dubbed themselves. All four of them had enlisted in the Navy at the end of that summer, and something had gone horribly wrong between Ford and Bree, ending their years-long friendship. I had some suspicions about what that might have been, but I'd never asked. Bree and I were friends, but not that kind of close. And even if we were, I wasn't sure she'd actually tell.

Lord knew I wasn't in any position to judge anybody for the way they chose to run their love life.

"Fair enough." I drained the last of my IPA. "I need to be getting on." I stood, shouldering my purse. "It's good to see you. Take care of yourself and Ed during the storm."

Bree saluted. "Same goes. See you on the other side."

TWO

DANIEL

My ass was asleep, and the numbness was creeping up my thighs. I shifted uncomfortably in my chair in the conference room at Nag's Head Coast Guard base, my new second home. The fluorescent lights buzzed overhead with that particular institutional hum that seemed to burrow into your skull after hours of exposure. At some dim, distant point in the past, this chair had been padded—probably when Reagan was in office, judging by the faded fabric and metal frame showing through at the corners. Years of briefings just like this one had broken it down to nothing but false promises of comfort.

Shipping routes and tracking data filled the massive screen mounted on the far wall, a spiderweb of coordinates and time-stamps that told the cold, hard facts of drug trafficking patterns in the Outer Banks. Red dots marked known drop points, yellow lines traced suspected routes, and blue zones indicated our patrol areas. It was a digital map of criminal enterprises, color-coded and sanitized for official consumption. The reason I was here, so far as the Coast Guard was concerned.

"And here's where we lost track of the vessel." Lieutenant Commander Hayes stepped closer to the screen, his laser pointer creating a red dot that danced across the display. He circled a blip that disappeared off the coast of Hatteras, somewhere in the maze of shoals and channels that made these waters a smuggler's paradise.

I leaned forward, elbows finding purchase on the scarred conference table that bore the ring stains of a thousand coffee cups. "We saw the same pattern operating in the Gulf. They're using the barrier islands as natural cover, probably making drops at night when visibility's low and the tourist boats have cleared out."

Across the table, a sheriff's deputy with graying temples and tired eyes scribbled notes in a composition book that looked like it had survived several hurricanes. Working as liaison between the Coast Guard and local law enforcement wasn't too different from my old post in Louisiana—just swap cypress swamps for salt marshes and Cajun accents for Outer Banks drawls. Drug runners were drug runners, whether they were slipping through bayous thick with Spanish moss or ducking between barrier islands dotted with wild horses.

"LaRue, what was your success rate with night interdiction operations in the Gulf?" Hayes asked, turning from the screen to fix me with the kind of stare that suggested he already knew the answer but wanted it on record.

"Thirty percent higher when we coordinated with local fishing boats and charter operations. They knew the water patterns, the seasonal changes, the hiding spots better than the traffickers ever could." I pulled up the statistical analysis from my last operation on my tablet, swiping through screens of data that represented months of planning and execution. "Small craft, crews familiar with every inch of shoreline, able to move quick and quiet through shallow water where our larger vessels couldn't follow."

The meeting dragged on with the relentless pace of bureaucracy at work. We'd already been grinding through this briefing for three hours, dissecting intercept strategies and resource allocation with the kind of methodical thoroughness that made my eyelids heavy. Charts and graphs blurred together as speakers droned about funding allocations and jurisdictional boundaries. I found my mind drifting south, past Oregon Inlet with its fishing fleet and charter boats, past the tourist spots clogged with rental houses and miniature golf courses, all the way down to Hatterwick Island where the development thinned out and the landscape turned wild again.

Gabi was down there somewhere, probably finishing up her afternoon appointments at the island clinic. I checked my watch—4:20 PM. She might be wrapping up with her last patient, updating charts in that careful handwriting. Or maybe she was already off work. Would she be stopping by her family's place for dinner? Out with friends at whatever passed for nightlife on an island with two thousand residents? I didn't know what her routine looked like now, and that ignorance sat in my chest like a stone.

Because it had been three months since I'd taken that promotion to Seattle without talking to her first. Three months of gray skies and rain that never seemed to stop, of realizing what a complete and utter idiot I was. Three months of staring at her contact information in my phone and not knowing what words could possibly make up for the way I'd handled things.

Getting this transfer to the Outer Banks hadn't been easy. I'd called in just about every favor anyone had ever owed me, worked connections from my Gulf Coast drug task force days where I'd done the solid, reliable work that earned me that

Seattle promotion in the first place. Burned a bridge or two with supervisors who'd expected me to stay put and be grateful for the career advancement. The work here was important—these waters were becoming a major trafficking corridor as enforcement tightened elsewhere along the coast. But if I was being honest with myself—and I was trying to be these days—breaking up drug operations wasn't the primary reason I'd fought so hard for this posting.

I glanced at my phone, the screen reflecting the harsh conference room lighting. No messages. No missed calls. And why would there be? She hadn't responded to any of the texts I'd sent from Seattle—carefully worded attempts at conversation that had gone unanswered until I'd finally stopped sending them. I hadn't told her I was here, hadn't told her I was coming at all. I'd thought this was the kind of gesture better made in person, so she could see in my face how serious I was about making things right. But now, sitting in this sterile room with drug interdiction statistics scrolling past, I wondered if I'd just made another miscalculation.

Fixing things with Gabi would be infinitely harder than tracking down smugglers in the dark. At least with smugglers, I understood the patterns, could predict their moves based on weather and tides and market pressures. With Gabi... I'd already made the wrong move once. I couldn't afford another mistake, not when there might not be a third chance.

It was so damn easy to picture her the way she'd been during those long weekends in New Orleans during her residency. Perched cross-legged on that narrow balcony overlooking Royal Street, still in her wrinkled scrubs after a thirty-six-hour rotation at Tulane Medical Center, her dark hair escaping from the practical braid she wore for work and curling around her face in the heavy Louisiana humidity. I'd bring her beignets from Café du Monde and coffee strong enough to wake the dead, and we'd sit there talking about everything and nothing while the city slowly came alive below us. Medical school stories and Coast Guard adventures, family gossip and half-formed dreams about the future. It had been such a comfortable routine, so natural and easy that I hadn't realized how much I'd come to depend on it until it was gone.

"These coordinates match the pattern from three previous incidents." Hayes's voice cut through my memories like a foghorn, yanking me back to the present with uncomfortable suddenness.

Work. Right. Focus on the job. This was what I was supposedly good at—uncovering patterns in criminal behavior, anticipating moves, coordinating assets across multiple agencies. Give me a maritime chess game with drug runners any day of the week. At least that was a problem I knew how to solve. But telling the woman I loved that I'd screwed up beyond belief? Acknowledging that I'd taken her for granted and made a major life decision without considering how it would affect her? Well, I'd rather board a hostile vessel in twenty-foot swells during a gale.

The conference room door burst open with enough force to rattle the frame. Chief Weather Officer Lopez stepped in, tablet clutched in her hands and an expression that immediately put everyone on alert. "Sir, urgent update on Hurricane Hannah. The track's shifted significantly."

Hayes straightened in his chair. "Where's she headed now?"

"Direct hit on the Outer Banks, making landfall in forty-eight hours. Current projections show Category 3, possibly strengthening to 4 before landfall." Lopez swiped her tablet, pulling up the latest satellite imagery. "Hatterwick's right at the edge of the cone of uncertainty."

My stomach clenched like I'd taken a punch. Hatterwick. Gabi. Two thousand people on a barrier island with one main road and limited evacuation options, staring down a major hurricane.

"Well, that changes our surveillance timeline considerably," Hayes said, his voice carrying the weight of someone mentally reshuffling priorities. "LaRue, what was standard Gulf protocol for pre-storm drug trafficking activity?"

I forced myself to focus on the tactical question, though part of my mind was already calculating wind speeds and storm surge projections. "Traffickers typically try to move product before severe weather hits. They can't risk losing millions in cargo to storm damage or having their boats trapped by high seas." I pulled up historical data from Hurricane Katrina and other major storms. "We usually saw a significant spike in movement twenty-four to thirty-six hours before landfall."

"So we've got maybe a day, possibly less, to catch them before Hannah shuts down all marine operations. Given how this particular operation has been developing, that timeline seems optimistic at best."

I nodded, but my mind was already racing south across sixty nautical miles of increasingly choppy water. Under normal circumstances, that was nothing—an easy run in a fast boat. But with a hurricane bearing down, those miles might as well have been six hundred. I'd waited too long to make things right with Gabi, and now Mother Nature was about to decide for me.

Hayes pulled up the coastal emergency management map, marking mandatory evacuation zones in stark red overlays. "We'll need teams at key points along the coast to assist emergency services with evacuation coordination. LaRue, you're taking Echo team to Hatterwick Island."

My pulse quickened, adrenaline flooding my system, but I kept my expression carefully neutral. Professional. Just another assignment. "Copy that, sir. How much personnel are we talking?"

"Four-person team. Standard hurricane protocol—assist local authorities with evacuation coordination, help secure critical facilities, maintain emergency communications during and after the storm." He zoomed in on Hatterwick's outline, a narrow sliver of land that looked impossibly vulnerable against the vast ocean. "You'll set up operations at the fire station. They've got backup generators and the most structurally sound building on the island."

I noted the location on my own tablet, just off the main road that wound through Sutter's Ferry. Three blocks from the island's medical clinic, according to the map. Not that I'd memorized the layout of Gabi's workplace or anything.

"What happens to our trafficking surveillance operation?" Lopez asked, still clutching her weather data like a lifeline.

"Mother Nature's got other plans for us." Hayes closed the map display with a gesture that felt final. "We'll resume once Hannah passes and we can assess the damage. For now, priority one is storm preparation and civilian safety. Everything else is secondary."

The meeting wrapped with the usual flurry of logistical details—equipment load-outs, communication channels, transport schedules, fuel requirements. My team would deploy first thing in the morning. Just twelve hours until I'd be headed directly into Gabi's world, whether she wanted me there or not. I itched to leave sooner, both to check on her safety and because I suspected the compressed timeline might cause some of the drug runners to make mistakes in their rush to move product. But orders were orders, and preparation was everything in an operation like this.

Back at my desk in the bullpen, I pulled up Hatterwick Island's emergency response plan, a surprisingly comprehensive document for such a small community. One main road that circled the island's perimeter like a necklace. Two thousand year-round residents, though that number swelled to nearly ten thousand during peak summer months. Primary evacuation point is at the ferry terminal on the western shore. Medical services are coordinated through Island Medical Clinic, Dr. Paul Sibley, Chief Medical Officer. I paused at that entry, wondering if that was Gabi's boss.

"Ready for some island time, boss?" Petty Officer Peterson, my second-in-command, dropped a stack of weather reports on my desk with a thud that scattered my thoughts. He was grinning with the kind of enthusiasm that only came from someone who'd never ridden out a major hurricane on a barrier island.

"Just another deployment, Peterson." I closed the emergency response file and reached for the weather data. "Nothing we haven't handled before."

"You worked hurricane response in the Gulf, right? Should be similar setup?"

"This is smaller scale, which can be both good and bad." I stood up, stretching muscles cramped from too many hours in that miserable conference room chair. "Barrier islands can be tricky during major storms. Storm surge, flooding, limited access once the weather turns. We'll need to be completely self-sufficient."

"How long do you think we'll be stuck there?"

"Depends on the storm track and how much damage she does. " I pulled up the satellite view of Hatterwick again. "There's no bridge to the mainland, so they're more cut off than a lot of the Outer Banks if shit goes sideways."

A couple thousand people scattered across twenty-nine square miles of sand and marsh grass. One medical clinic where Gabi spent her days treating everything from fishing accidents to heart attacks. Finding her wouldn't be the challenge—hell, on an island that small, I'd probably run into her at the grocery store. No, the real challenge would be figuring out what to say when I did. How do you apologize for three months of silence? How do you explain that you finally understood what you'd thrown away?

I guess I had about twelve hours to figure that out.

THREE

GABI

I pulled into the crushed-shell driveway beside Hoyt's battered F-150. He'd bought it slightly used the summer I'd left for college and had put countless miles on it since as he and Caroline renovated this house, taking it from the run-down duplex he'd bought it to the home it was today. The late afternoon sun cast long shadows across the restored beach house, its weathered blue clapboard siding and white trim glowing in the golden light. Music and laughter drifted through the screened windows, as it often did. After a childhood where we'd all been forced to stay quiet, creeping around lest we set off our unpredictable father's temper, my sister made sure her own brood felt comfortable taking up space and making noise. Theirs was a house full of love. And it was home sweet temporary home.

At least until I found my own place.

Grabbing my medical bag from the passenger seat, I climbed the wooden steps to the wraparound porch. Through the front window, I caught glimpses of movement in the kitchen—Caroline's dark head bent over the stove, Hoyt's tall frame reaching into an upper cabinet. I hadn't missed dinner after all. At the front door, my hand hesitated on the knob. After ten hours of dealing with patients, I craved the quiet of my upstairs bedroom. But the faint scents of garlic and olive oil as I let myself inside prompted my stomach to growl loud enough to wake the dead.

"Look who finally made it home!" Caroline's voice rang out as I shut the door behind me.

I dropped my bag by the stairs and picked my way through a maze of toys in the living room, back to the spacious kitchen.

The room was warm and inviting, with an array of herbs growing in painted clay pots along the windowsill of the wide window that overlooked the dunes. Bright stainless steel pots hung from the ceiling rack over the rustic island that was the centerpiece of the space. It was the kind of kitchen Caroline had always wanted.

The woman herself wiped her hands on a dishtowel and turned to flash a bright smile my way. "I was starting to think we'd have to send out a search party."

"Clinic ran late, and I popped by the Brewhouse for a drink before I came home." I gave the air a sniff. "Is that albondigas?" The rich aroma of Mexican meatball soup made my mouth water.

"With extra cilantro, just how you like it." With one hand resting on the swell of her baby bump, Caroline stirred the pot with a wooden spoon. "And I made fresh tortillas because the little alien demanded it."

"Thanks to the little alien." I draped an arm around her shoulders. "You feeling okay? Not doing too much?"

"I'll have you know it's been a whole three days since I vomited. I think we're past the worst."

Hoyt and I exchanged knowing looks. With her previous two pregnancies, the morning sickness hadn't fully abated until the start of her third trimester.

The thundering of feet on the stairs rattled the hanging pots. "Tía Gabi!"

Audrey crashed into my legs, her dark curls wild around her face. Logan wasn't far behind, brandishing a crayon drawing. "Look what I made!"

I knelt down to properly admire the artwork—a surprisingly detailed fire truck rendered in red and yellow. "This is amazing, *mijo*."

"It's for Daddy's station!" Logan beamed, showing off the gap where his front teeth used to be.

The chaos and noise washed over me. Courtesy of that drink at the Brewhouse, I managed to smile instead of wince. I loved these two to pieces and never wanted to make them think otherwise.

"Alright, monsters, wash those hands if you want dinner." Hoyt's voice rang with the natural authority honed over years of firefighting. The kids scrambled toward the bathroom, shoving each other to be first.

"Need help with anything?" I moved to the cabinet for plates.

"Grab the sour cream from the fridge?" Caroline ladled the steaming soup into bowls, while Hoyt stacked still-warm tortillas on a plate lined with a bright, embroidered cloth.

The kids raced back, hands thrust out for inspection. "Clean enough?" Audrey wiggled her fingers.

"Pass inspection." Hoyt gave them each a playful salute. "Now help your tía set the table."

We moved around each other in the familiar dance of family dinner prep, the kids carefully carrying napkins and spoons while the adults handled the hot dishes. The kitchen filled with steam from the soup, the smell of fresh tortillas, and the sound of happy chatter.

Once we settled at the table, Caroline passed me a warm tortilla. "How was your day?"

I tore off a piece and dunked it in my soup. "Busy. Everyone's coming in for last-minute prescriptions before the storm. Not that it'll make much difference if it hits before the pharmacy has a chance to restock." That was the reality of being on an island. We didn't necessarily have access to everything all the time, and when weather cut us off from the mainland, we made do. "I put in an extra order myself, but I don't know if it'll make it in on the last ferry or not."

"Smart thinking ahead." Hoyt helped Logan cut his meatballs into smaller pieces. "Chief's got us doing inventory checks at the station. Making sure all the generators are fueled up, chainsaws are sharp."

"Speaking of prep..." Caroline shot her husband a look. "When are you putting up our shutters?"

"Tomorrow morning before shift. Already got the brackets cleaned out yesterday." He reached across the table to wipe sauce from Audrey's chin. "Though honestly, you should just pack up and head to Mom and Dad's tonight. No point waiting."

"We'll go tomorrow after you finish the shutters." Caroline's tone brooked no argument. "I want to make sure everything's secured first."

I stirred my soup. "Need help with anything? I can come by after clinic hours."

"Got it covered, sis." Caroline squeezed my hand. "You focus on the medical center prep. How many patients are staying through the storm?"

"Thankfully, none. So far, anyway." Our clinic could house up to four patients for the short term, but we weren't a hospital. Anything more serious than could be dealt with on site was sent to bigger facilities on the mainland or up at Nag's Head. I hoped none of those beds became necessary in the wake of the hurricane. "Either way, we've got the generator ready and enough supplies to get us through up to a week, depending on circumstances. And I'm coordinating with some of my staff and the EMTs from the fire station to set up a makeshift clinic at the community center, in case it's needed."

"Smart thinking. Coast Guard's sending a team down tomorrow too," Hoyt said between bites. "They're bunking at the station while they help with prep. Chief's got them doing door-to-door checks with us, making sure everyone's got evacuation plans. and whatnot."

My spoon clattered against the bowl. Heat crept up my neck as three pairs of eyes turned to me.

"Sorry." I picked up my spoon, focusing on the chunks of potato floating in my soup. My heart thudded against my ribs.

Don't be ridiculous, I ordered myself. It was completely normal for the Coast Guard to help during a hurricane. It wasn't like I'd be seeing *that* particular Coastguardsman. He was on the other side of the country, living his best life without me. There was no reason whatsoever for me to feel like I'd just been punched in the stomach.

"Gabi?" Caroline's voice was soft, concern etched across her features. "You okay?"

"Just tired." I pushed back from the table, my appetite vanishing. "Think I'm gonna head up. Tomorrow's going to be crazy at the clinic."

Caroline frowned. "You haven't finished your soup."

"I ate some appetizers at the Brewhouse." The lie tasted bitter on my tongue. "Really, I'm fine. Just need some sleep."

"Want me to save you a bowl for later?" Caroline's dark eyes studied my face.

"Please." I kissed the top of her head, then bent to hug the kids. "Goodnight monsters. Be good for your mama."

"Night Tía!" they chorused.

I took my bowl to the sink, then retreated. My medical bag was where I'd left it by the stairs. I grabbed it, going up two steps at a time. In my room, I closed the door and leaned against it, letting out a shaky breath.

Hurricane Daniel. That wasn't the actual name of the storm that had trapped me in a stairwell during my second year of residency, during the worst storm to hit New Orleans since Katrina. But it was how I thought of the man who'd been there to keep me sane during those long hours. Because he'd swept into my carefully ordered life like a category five hurricane and disrupted everything before blowing back out again, leaving nothing but wreckage in his wake.

My head dropped back against the door as the memories flooded in with the force of a storm surge. How the wind had howled outside that concrete tunnel like a living thing, as rain pelted the building in sheets so thick you couldn't see two feet past the windows. The emergency lighting had cast everything in an eerie red glow, and I'd been fighting full-blown panic when Daniel appeared—tall, broad-shouldered, radiating the kind of calm competence that made you believe everything would be okay.

His steady voice with that hypnotic Louisiana drawl had a Cajun edge that wrapped around each word like honey, walking me through Coast Guard protocol, explaining how they tracked storms and predicted their paths. The way his hands had sketched patterns in the air as he detailed wind rotation and pressure systems, those long fingers moving with such precision and grace that I'd found myself mesmerized despite my fear. He'd made meteorology sound like poetry, turning technical jargon into something beautiful and understandable.

The power had flickered once, twice, then died completely, plunging us into absolute darkness. And his fingers had found mine in that black void, strong and warm and callused from years of rope work, giving me an anchor in the storm when I felt like I might float away on a tide of terror. I'd turned toward him as the only stable thing in a world gone mad, and somehow our mouths had brushed in the darkness. An accident at first, a collision of breath and uncertainty. Then, so very much not an accident as we'd dove at each other with desperate hunger, his hands tangling in my hair as he'd pressed me back against the cold concrete wall and made me forget about everything but the storm he stirred inside me.

I shoved away from the door, pacing my small room like a caged animal. The hardwood floors that Caroline had lovingly refinished creaked under my restless steps. It hardly mattered anymore, I told myself fiercely. That kiss that had tasted like coffee and promises. The time that followed, when we'd spent every spare moment together—him showing me hidden corners of the French Quarter, me stealing him away to quiet cafes where we could talk for hours about everything and nothing. None of it had meant enough to make him stay. Or even discuss staying with me, like I was someone whose feelings mattered.

He'd just announced one day, casual as you please, that he'd been promoted and was moving to Seattle. As if my opinion, our relationship, the way I'd whispered his name in the dark—hadn't factored into his decision at all. And no matter how he'd acted during those stolen months, how he'd held me like I was precious, I knew it had been a choice. He'd chosen his career over me without even the courtesy of a real conversation about it.

The wood floor creaked beneath my bare feet as I prowled to the window, my reflection a pale ghost in the glass. Beyond, beach grasses whipped in the strengthening wind like dancers gone wild, bending nearly horizontal before snapping back upright. The ocean was already showing whitecaps, waves building as they rolled toward shore. Another storm was coming, and part of me welcomed it. At least natural disasters were honest about the destruction they brought.

But I'd weather it just fine, I reminded myself, squaring my shoulders against the phantom weight of old heartbreak. I was a Carrera, after all. We'd survived everything life had thrown at us—an abusive father who'd used his fists more than his words, the devastating loss of our mother when we were still so young, crushing medical school debt that would follow me for years. A broken heart that had taught me never to trust a man in uniform again. What was one more hurricane in the face of all that? At least this time, I knew the storm was coming.

FOUR

DANIEL

The rumble of the Zodiac's engines cut through the morning calm as we made our way down the Atlantic side of the Outer Banks to Hatterwick Island, the furthest Southern tip of the chain of barrier islands that ran along the North Carolina coast. At last. I wished the trip was for the personal reasons that had drawn me across the country to begin with, but if I wanted the opportunity to stay, my duty had to come first.

With the hurricane inbound, our official mission today was part patrol, part storm prep and evacuation assistance, but I was keeping my eyes peeled for any evidence of the drug runners hoofing it to move product before the storm hit. The inevitable chaos that frequently surrounded evacuations could provide good cover. But with less than forty-eight hours until Hannah was due to make landfall, the pressure was on, and that could likewise lead to mistakes. I could only hope to be fortunate enough to be able to execute both pieces of my mission while I was down here. It could never hurt to impress the brass.

"Skipper, I've got a flashing light at ten o'clock," Vance called out over the din.

I looked to the left and spotted the distant flicker of a signaling lamp. "Let's check it out."

Angling toward the light, I bumped up our speed, cutting through the swells. As we approached, the sleek lines of a stranded sailboat came into view, sails luffing uselessly. A single sailor stood on the decks, waving at our approach. Legitimate distress, or could this guy be waiting out here to make some kind of transfer of goods?

"Look alive, y'all. Be ready for anything." I pulled the Zodiac alongside and throttled back the engines.

The sailor, a middle-aged man with a weather-worn face and silver at his temples, curled his hands around the rail. "Y'all are a sight for sore eyes. Engine gave out. I was trying to make it back before the storm, but I didn't get far."

"Headed to Hatterwick?" I asked.

"To the marina there, yeah."

Courtesy of the surveillance photos we'd been studying in our task force meetings, I knew where that was. "We'll give you a tow."

Peterson helped secure the line, and we turned toward the marina on the southwest tip of the island.

After three weeks of studying charts and aerial photos from our task force meetings, I expected it to look more familiar than it did. But two-dimensional tactical representations could never capture the soul of a place. The island rose up from the waves, a long, low shape with the green of maritime forests as a backdrop to the mega-houses that marched along the coast like colorful jewels. But on the otherwise empty beach just to the north, I saw a cluster of dark shapes moving along the shoreline. The wild horses Hatterwick was known for, I assumed. I'd seen them marked on our patrol maps as a local wildlife consideration, but seeing them in person was different. I wished we had time for a closer inspection, but there was work to be done. God and a good grovel willing, I'd be spending a lot more time down here in the future, and there'd be another opportunity..

We delivered the sailboat to the harbor, getting it back to its slip and secured before we moored our own vessel. Echo team gathered our gear, and we made our way into Sutter's Ferry to check in at the fire station since it was our designated command post for the duration. Despite being team lead, I hung back a bit, letting Vance take point. No need to draw attention to myself just yet.

The village itself was laid out more or less in a grid, with a main thoroughfare following the curve of the harbor that faced Pamlico Sound and the distant mainland. We kept to the sidewalk, walking past dive shops, fishing supply stores, restaurants, and a whole host of tourist shops with kitschy names like Tides and Trifles, Ocean Oddities, and Seas the Day. Were any of these fronts for moving product other than tourist souvenirs? Drop sites? That was the kind of thing we needed boots on the ground to uncover. After the hurricane was past, I intended to make the recommendation that we embed a few men under-cover to better make such an assessment. I hoped like hell I'd be one of them, and that it would give me a chance to make things up to Gabi. But one thing at a time.

The streets and sidewalks were teeming with people, a chaotic mix of urgency and barely controlled panic. Despite the fact that I wasn't a native to these waters, it was easy as breathing to tell the tourists from the locals based on the frenetic, almost manic energy surrounding the former as they made last-minute stops at every shop they passed, arms loaded with unnecessary purchases, and gathered up their belongings before heading to catch one of the last ferry runs off the island before Hannah made landfall.

The tourists moved with the jerky, inefficient movements of people who had no real plan beyond "get off this island right now." They clutched overstuffed bags, dragged wheeled suitcases that caught on every crack in the sidewalk, and kept checking their phones as if the weather apps might suddenly deliver better news. Their faces held that particular brand of vacation-ruined panic—the appearance of people who'd paid good money for a beach getaway and were now fleeing for their lives.

The locals, by contrast, moved with purpose. They knew where they were going and what they needed to do. Their movements were economical, practiced. These were people who'd weathered storms before and understood the difference between prudent preparation and pointless panic.

I found myself hoping like hell that the ferry company had enough ships running and enough time remaining to get everyone off-island who wanted to leave. The alternative of being trapped here with a bunch of panicked tourists during a Category 3 hurricane wasn't something any of us wanted to deal with on top of everything else.

Vance hooked a sharp left, leading us back toward the sound side of the village. According to the detailed map I'd memorized during our briefing, the island clinic where Gabi worked was three blocks east of our current position. Not that I was counting blocks or plotting routes in my head. There'd be time to head in that direction once we'd established our command presence and coordinated with local emergency services. Mission first, personal business second. That was how it had to be, no matter how much every instinct I had was screaming at me to lay eyes on her.

The fire station stood on a prominent corner lot, a tidy clapboard building that spoke to the community's pride in their emergency services. The main section rose a full two stories, with three equipment bays that marched across the front in perfect symmetry. A taller wing that housed the living quarters and administrative offices sat at the far end, its multi-paned windows set at even intervals in the pale blue siding that had been recently painted. The whole place was impeccably maintained and surprisingly inviting, as such municipal buildings went. Even under normal circumstances, this would have been an impressive facility for a community of only two thousand souls.

A crew of firefighters was already hard at work installing heavy-duty hurricane shutters over the windows, their movements efficient and coordinated. The metallic clang of shutters being secured echoed across the street, punctuated by the occasional shout of instruction.

Good. That meant less preparatory work for my team, and more time to focus on our actual mission objectives—both the official ones and the decidedly unofficial one that had my stomach in knots.

We ducked inside through the first open bay, the familiar scent of diesel fuel, rubber, and cleaning chemicals hitting my nostrils. The space buzzed with controlled activity. It seemed like men were everywhere—checking over equipment with methodical precision, testing radio communications, reviewing emergency protocols. Hurricane preparation was already in full swing around here, which would make squeezing in any covert surveillance work considerably more challenging. But we'd adapt. We always did. And we'd see what opportunities presented themselves once the immediate crisis had passed.

A dark-haired guy in turnout pants and a department t-shirt broke away from a group examining a pump truck and headed toward us, his stride confident and purposeful. Something about his bearing marked him as someone in authority, even before he spoke.

"Can I help y'all?" His accent carried a distinctive Outer

Banks flavor—not quite Southern, not quite Mid-Atlantic, but something uniquely coastal.

I stepped forward and extended my hand in a firm grip. "Petty Officer First Class Daniel LaRue of the United States Coast Guard. I'm here to meet with your fire chief about how my team can best assist with storm preparation and emergency response coordination."

"Chief Thompson's off-site for an emergency planning meeting with the chief of police and the mayor, but I'm Captain Hoyt McNamara. Good to have y'all here. The extra hands and expertise are much appreciated, especially with the timeline we're working under."

My gaze sharpened on McNamara as I introduced Peters, Vance, Rawlings, and Martinez, each man stepping forward with professional courtesy. I recognized that name. This was Gabi's brother-in-law, married to her older sister. Did he know about me? About what had happened between Gabi and me back in New Orleans? About how spectacularly I'd managed to screw things up?

His expression remained professionally neutral and welcoming, giving nothing away. Either Gabi hadn't mentioned me to her family—which was entirely possible, given how things had ended—or McNamara was considerably better at hiding his personal thoughts than most people. Either scenario left me walking a tightrope. If he didn't know about me, I wanted to keep it that way until I'd had a chance to talk to Gabi first. And if he did know, well, given the protective nature of most families, he might be more inclined to plant his fist in my face than welcome my assistance. For now, I'd keep things strictly professional and see how the wind blew.

"You ever been through a hurricane before, LaRue?" McNamara asked, his tone conversational but assessing.

"Plenty of them. I'm a bayou boy, born and bred down in

Louisiana. I'm just recently posted to the Nag's Head station, so this'll be my first Atlantic hurricane. Used to them sweeping up from the Gulf of Mexico, but I don't expect the fundamentals are much different here than they were back home."

I watched his face for any flicker of recognition, any sign that the mention of Louisiana might have triggered a memory of conversations with Gabi. But there wasn't so much as a twitch.

"Was that where you were stationed before? Louisiana?"

"Came from a brief posting out in Seattle." The posting that was supposed to have been the making of my career, the golden opportunity I'd been too stupid to recognize for the trap it was. "But before that, I worked Gulf Coast drug interdiction operations for several years. Saw my fair share of storms down there, from tropical depressions all the way up to Category 5 monsters."

"Seattle's a long damned way from the South." Something in his tone suggested he understood exactly how far away that really was—not just in miles, but in culture, climate, and everything that made a place feel like home.

I flashed him an easy grin and let a little more bayou slip into my voice, the accent I'd spent years learning to dial back for professional advancement. "You ain't wrong about that. I surely do appreciate being back in the South, where everybody understands that the default when you say 'tea' is sweet and iced, and they actually know how to make it proper instead of serving you some bitter leaf water with a packet of sugar on the side."

McNamara's laugh was genuine, the kind of shared understanding that passed between people who'd both suffered through bad tea in foreign territories. "Amen to that, brother. How long do we have y'all for?"

"For the duration of the emergency. We're equipped and

authorized to assist with evacuation coordination, facility security, and emergency communications infrastructure." I gestured toward our gear, neatly organized and clearly substantial. "Brought our own supplies and equipment, so we won't be taxing your local resources or getting in your way."

"Much appreciated. I heard there's already been two separate brawls at the island market this morning over supplies. People fighting over the last roll of toilet paper like it's gonna save anybody from having their roof ripped clean off their house."

"There's something about weather panic that always makes people lose their damn minds over toilet paper, bread, and milk." I flashed him a wry, knowing smile. "Like they're planning to make the world's most depressing French toast while they wait out the apocalypse."

McNamara chuckled at that, and I could see some of the tension ease from his shoulders. Good. Building rapport with local emergency personnel was always crucial, but in this case, it carried extra weight.

"You got family riding things out here on the island?" I asked, keeping my tone casual, professionally curious. Just one emergency responder asking another about personal logistics that might affect operational availability.

"My wife's pregnant with our third child. She and our kids are planning to ride things out with my parents here on Hatterwick, so that frees me up to deal with whatever crisis management we need to handle." His voice carried the particular mix of pride and worry that came with being responsible for both a family and a community in danger.

Nothing was mentioned about his sister-in-law. Was Gabi planning to evacuate with the tourists and seasonal residents? Was she staying to help with medical emergencies? Working at the clinic through the storm? According to our briefing materials, the island clinic was designated as essential services and would remain operational throughout the emergency. She'd most likely be there, putting herself at risk to help others, because that was the kind of person she was. Not that I could ask about her without raising questions I wasn't remotely ready to answer.

Forcing myself to lock that particular curiosity away for later, I clapped my hands together with professional enthusiasm. "Well then, put us to work, Captain. The clock's ticking, and we've got a lot to accomplish before Hannah decides to pay y'all a visit."

FIVE

GABI

"Good morning, islanders! This is Sam Lewis of WHAT radio, the official radio station of Hatterwick Island, with your storm update. Hurricane Hannah continues to churn in the Atlantic and is still projected to make landfall on the Outer Banks sometime tomorrow afternoon or evening, with the potential to be a Category 3 storm."

With a sigh, I turned up the volume on my car radio as I backed out of my sister's driveway and headed toward Sutter's Ferry. The village was going to be a madhouse, with people fleeing like rats from a sinking ship.

"We want to remind all residents and tourists who plan to evacuate the island to please do so today. The last ferry departing Hatterwick will be at 3pm sharp. Evacuation is strongly recommended but not mandatory for all non-essential personnel."

More people would stay than go. That was the way of things here. We were hardier than most storms, which was why our village had survived in some form or another for more than a century.

On the radio, Sam continued, "For those staying on the island, sandbags are still available behind Town Hall until noon or whenever supplies run out. All residents should be finalizing storm preparations and have emergency kits ready. Expect powerful winds, flooding rains, and storm surge up to fifteen feet in vulnerable areas. We'll continue to keep you updated on Hurricane Hannah's track and intensity as it approaches. Stay tuned to WHAT for all the latest storm news. Be safe out there, Hatterwick!"

For at least the dozenth time, I cursed the crap timing of Dr. Sibley's vacation to Mexico. The idea of being the only doctor on-island for this made me nervous. Not that I wasn't capable, but depending on how the storm went down, there might be greater need than I could manage as just one person. I was praying for the best and otherwise bracing myself for a total shitshow.

Despite the relatively early hour, as I hit the edge of the village proper, I could see evidence of the news spreading. Streets were clogged with vehicles as tourists fled toward the ferry terminal that would get them back to the mainland. Locals were easy to pick out. They stood outside homes and buildings, boarding over windows or installing hurricane shutters. Others would be gathering supplies and planning hurricane parties. Me, I'd be making sure that the clinic was ready for whatever emergency came our way as a result of storm prep or the aftermath.

Because of the congested roads, I was later than I intended when I pulled behind the clapboard building housing the clinic. Nina was just slipping out of her car, her myriad of tiny braids gathered into a thicker plait that hung over one shoulder. She flashed a bright smile that stood out against her medium brown skin.

"Mornin', Doc. Looks like it's gonna be a nasty one."

We both looked off to the south, where clouds were already beginning to build in the distance. "I think they're wrong about when it's gonna hit. We're gonna get somethin' sooner."

"Hope not. Lotta folks still tryin' to get off-island. Rather not have to find a place for them."

Or spend all our storm supplies. Not that we'd begrudge them aid if needed, but despite some of the monster houses marching along our coastline, in general, our island wasn't exactly rolling in money and assets. Because we depended heavily on tourist dollars, we tolerated the annual invasion of our shores with varying degrees of hospitality, but there was no quicker way to draw a line between us and them than the kind of storm that would dry those tourist dollars up for a stretch. That and no islander wanted to be responsible for idiot mainlanders who didn't have the first clue how to prepare for or ride out a storm like this.

"Here's hoping they get off-island as planned," I said, though I had my doubts about the timing.

We strode up the weathered wooden stairs toward the back entrance of the clinic. Like most buildings scattered across Hatterwick, the structure was elevated on sturdy concrete stilts —a necessary precaution against the relentless storm surges and seasonal flooding that came with our coastal location. The morning air already carried that heavy, electric feeling that preceded big weather, and I could taste the salt spray being whipped up from the increasingly agitated ocean.

"Are you planning on keeping us open regular hours today?" Nina's voice carried a note of concern as she glanced toward the darkening southern horizon.

"Depends on what comes in, I guess." I shifted my medical bag to my other shoulder, already mentally cataloging our supplies and staffing for what was bound to be a challenging day. "You and I both know we're gonna get more people in for accidents from the storm prep—folks falling off ladders while securing shutters, cuts from boarding up windows, that sort of thing. We'll be keeping an eye on the weather reports."

At the door, I paused, my hand disappearing deep into the depths of my oversized purse as I fumbled for my keys. Something about the entrance looked... off.

"Something wrong?" Nina stepped closer and followed my gaze.

I stared at the door knob, taking in the fresh scratches gouged deep into the metal all around its circumference. The hardware itself appeared loose, a little askew in its mounting, as if someone had tried to wrench it clean off the door. "Somebody tried to jimmy the back door."

"Oh, shit!" Nina's voice pitched higher with alarm. "Do you think they got anything?"

I leaned in for a closer examination without touching anything, noting the way the wood around the lock mechanism showed fresh scrapes and gouges. "Doesn't look like they actually got in." But the very fact that someone had made the attempt sent an uncomfortable chill down my spine—especially with a hurricane bearing down on us and the island about to be in chaos.

Other than Morrison's Pharmacy on Main Street, our clinic was the only medical facility on the island, which made us the sole source of prescription medications for miles around. We maintained strict protocols and didn't keep any Schedule-One narcotics on hand for precisely this reason, but your average desperate thief breaking into a medical facility might not know or care about such distinctions.

Pi pulled my cell phone from my pocket. "Do you feel safe running around to the front to check that door?"

Nina uncapped the mini-mace canister attached to her keychain. "Got it covered."

As she disappeared around the corner of the building, her footsteps crunching on the gravel pathway, I dialed 911.

"911 dispatch. What is your emergency?"

"This is Dr. Gabriella Carrera calling from the island clinic on Pelican Way. There's evidence that someone attempted to break in sometime since we closed last night."

"Is the door currently open, ma'am?"

"No, it's still closed. I haven't touched anything yet because I don't know if it's actually unlocked or not. My initial assessment is that they weren't able to gain entry, but I can't be certain without a proper examination."

Nina reappeared around the corner, giving me an enthusiastic thumbs up and calling out, "Front door looks normal!"

I relayed the information to the dispatcher. "The front entrance appears to be untouched."

"Please remain outside the building until an officer arrives. I'm dispatching someone to your location now."

"Understood. We'll wait out here."

Nina and I retreated to our respective vehicles in the small staff parking area, settling in to wait. The morning was growing warmer despite the threatening clouds, and I found myself checking my watch every few minutes, thinking about all the patients who might need us today.

Kristie Turner pulled her bright yellow Mini Cooper into the cramped staff lot, her late-thirties energy apparent as she bounded out of the driver's seat. She took one look at us sitting in our cars and called out with characteristic humor, "Are we having some kind of pre-hurricane party in the parking lot this morning?"

"Attempted break-in." I gestured toward the clinic's back entrance. "We're waiting for the police to clear the building."

"Well, damn." Kristie pushed her shoulder-length blonde hair back from her face and glanced at her watch. "Guess that means we're gonna be late opening this morning. Does this give me enough time to make a quick run to Panadería de la Isla for some pastries?"

The mention of Marisol's bakery made my stomach rumble, reminding me that I'd skipped breakfast in my rush to get to work early. I dug through my bag for my wallet, pulling out a twenty-dollar bill. "You know what? It's gonna be a hell of a long day with this storm coming. Get some treats for all of us."

"You want your usual empanada?" Kristie asked, already jingling her car keys.

I shook my head, feeling the stress of the morning settling into my shoulders. "Not sure a breakfast empanada is going to cut it today. I need sugar—real sugar. Get me as much as you can manage for twenty bucks."

She grinned, her eyes sparkling with mischief. "Consider it done, Doc."

A few minutes after Kristie drove off, a familiar police cruiser pulled into the lot. Officer Cory Teague emerged from the driver's seat, his tall frame unfolding as he adjusted his duty belt. Even after all these years, seeing him in uniform still felt a bit surreal—I could still picture him as the lanky high school senior who'd been a year ahead of me, more interested in surfing than law enforcement.

"Morning, Gabi," His easy coastal drawl marked him as a true islander. "Nina said y'all had a little trouble here?"

I gestured toward the clinic's back entrance, where the damage was visible even from several feet away. "I don't know if they managed to get inside or not. We haven't touched anything, figured you might want to dust for prints or whatever it is you do."

"Smart thinking." Cory nodded in approval, then turned to Nina. "You mentioned the front entrance wasn't disturbed?"

"That's right," Nina confirmed, stepping closer to join our

conversation. "Front door was still locked tight, and there weren't any scratches or damage that I could see. Doesn't look like they even tried anything there."

"Makes sense." Cory pulled a small digital camera from his belt. "Since the front faces the street, they'd be taking a big risk of being spotted. Y'all got any security cameras covering this back area?"

"No. That's obviously something we need to address." I made a mental note, but any major security upgrades would have to wait for Dr. Sibley's return from his vacation.

Cory went about his work methodically, documenting everything with photographs from multiple angles before pulling on latex gloves and testing the door handle. It turned freely but the door remained closed—still locked tight.

Once I'd unlocked the entrance with my key, Cory insisted on preceding us inside, systematically clearing each room of the modest clinic building.

"Everything looks secure in here," he announced.

He waited while I conducted my own inspection, checking our medical supplies cabinet, the locked medication storage, and the small safe where we kept emergency cash. "Nothing seems to be missing," I reported with relief.

"Well, that's good news." Cory closed his notebook with a satisfied snap. "In cases like this, no news really is the best possible outcome."

"You're not going to bother dusting for prints, are you?" I suspected I already knew the answer.

"I could go through the motions, but since that's the door your entire staff uses multiple times every day, any prints are going to be muddled. And considering that whoever did this didn't actually manage to gain entry, and we don't have any video evidence linking anyone to this door last night, there's not much more we can pursue. Especially with everyone on the island busy preparing for Hurricane Hannah."

"That's more or less what I figured you'd say. I mainly wanted to get it documented, just in case of... whatever might happen next." The thought that troubled me most was that if someone had attempted this once, they might very well try again during the storm when they assumed the building would be completely abandoned.

"Absolutely the right call," Cory assured me, tucking his notebook back into his uniform pocket. "I'll make sure this report is properly filed. And y'all might seriously want to consider upgrading that lock or adding a deadbolt before the next time you close up."

Right. Because we had unlimited time and resources to deal with hardware upgrades while the entire island was frantically preparing for a major hurricane. But I simply nodded. "I really appreciate you coming out so fast, Cory. Please stay safe out there today."

"You too, Gabi. Y'all are gonna be busy."

Kristie returned just as Cory was pulling out of the parking lot, her Mini Cooper loaded with the sweet, yeasty aromas of fresh pastries from Marisol's bakery. At almost the same moment, Justin Humphries, our other nurse scheduled for today, arrived in his beat-up pickup truck.

He climbed out slowly, his eyebrows raised as he took in the scene—Kristie with her arms full of bakery boxes, me standing by the clinic entrance, and the lingering presence of official police business hanging in the air.

"I take one day off and come back to find police cars in the parking lot?" Justin drawled, his voice carrying that particular blend of curiosity and concern that came from years of working in emergency medicine. "Is there somethin' important I need to know about?"

"Attempted break-in sometime last night," I explained, already moving toward the clinic entrance. "Whoever it was failed to get inside, but we'll discuss all the details during our staff meeting later. Right now, though, come grab one of Kristie's pastries and let's get these doors open to the public. I can already see folks starting to line up outside, and something tells me this is going to be one very long day."

SIX

DANIEL

The hammer's rhythm matched the thud of country music spilling from Home Port's open door. We'd been boarding up windows for the past three hours, and my shoulders burned from the repetitive motion. The dive bar was our last stop before a much-needed break.

"Ain't gonna be much view left when we're done." Tank, the aptly nicknamed big bruiser of a firefighter I'd been paired with, drove another nail into the plywood. "Though most folks come here for the beer, not the scenery."

A burst of laughter erupted from inside. The place was packed wall-to-wall with fishermen and dock workers, their voices a constant rumble beneath Merle Haggard's twang.

"Busy for lunch hour, considering the circumstances," I said, wiping sweat from my forehead with my sleeve.

"Hurricane's coming. Not like anybody's gonna be out on the water fishing in this weather. Everyone's getting their drinking in early." Tank grinned. "Plus, Jimmy makes the best burgers on the island. Better grab one while you can—place'll be closed once the storm hits."

My stomach growled on cue. We'd covered half the commercial district since morning, and all I'd had since I'd left Nag's Head at o'dark thirty was a single cup of firehouse coffee. The smell of grilled meat and fried food drifted out, making my mouth water.

"How many windows left?"

Tank counted under his breath. "Four on this side, two round back. Could probably use a breakthrough. These boards ain't going anywhere."

I set down my hammer and flexed my fingers. The skin on my palms was red and raw despite my work gloves.

"Lead the way." I followed Tank inside, blinking as my eyes adjusted to the dim interior. The place had that lived-in feel of a real local joint—fishing nets on the walls, dollar bills pinned to the ceiling, initials carved into the wooden tables. A few heads turned our way, but most folks were focused on their plates or conversations. This was exactly the kind of place I'd hoped to land to pick up some prospective intel.

We found two empty stools at the bar, wedging ourselves between a weathered fisherman nursing a beer and a dock worker still in his oil-stained coveralls. Tank waved to the bartender with the easy familiarity of someone who'd spent plenty of time on this barstool. "Jimmy! Two of your famous burgers. And whatever's cold and nonalcoholic."

Jimmy, a grizzled man with arms like tree trunks and a gray beard that had seen better days, slid two sweet teas our way without missing a beat. The glasses were already sweating in the humid air, condensation pooling on the scarred wooden bar top. Tank launched into an animated story about the current standings of the prank war that evidently was a staple around the fire station—something involving shaving cream in boots and plastic wrap over toilet seats.

I sipped the cool, refreshing drink and let the conversations wash over me, picking out threads of worried voices beneath the twang of country music. The sweet tea was perfectly brewed, with just enough sugar to cut through the heat and humidity that seemed to seep through even the boarded-up windows.

"—gonna be worse than Isabel, mark my words."

"Them folks up at Corolla are already heading inland..."

"—best get the boat up on blocks before..."

The conversations layered over each other like waves, creating a constant murmur of anxiety beneath Tank's increasingly elaborate tale of revenge plots. Everyone in the place vibrated with the restless energy that came before a big storm— the kind of nervous tension that made people drink a little faster and talk a little louder.

A gruff voice two stools down caught my attention, cutting through Tank's story like a knife. "Told you I saw lights out there last night. No reason for anybody to be running dark this close to shore."

My ears perked up at those words, but I kept my eyes on my drink, watching the ice cubes shift and melt. Running dark meant no navigation lights—illegal and dangerous, especially with a storm brewing. Could be nothing. Probably was nothing. But it could be everything. Down in the Gulf, cartels loved using hurricane chaos as cover. Less Coast Guard presence, fewer patrol boats, easier to slip past while everyone focused on evacuation and rescue ops.

I shifted slightly on my stool to better eavesdrop on their conversation without being obvious about it. Tank was still going on about the elaborate retaliation planned for whoever had filled Chief Morrison's coffee cup with salt—had he really said they were considering mayo in socks as payback?—which gave me perfect cover to eavesdrop on the more interesting conversation happening down the bar.

"Where'd you spot them?" the man's drinking buddy asked, his voice carrying the slow cadence of someone who'd spent his whole life on these waters.

"Out past the shoals. One, maybe two boats. Thought they might be part of that fishing fleet from Ocracoke at first, but they were running too close together. And silent."

Silent running. Another red flag waving in my mental periphery. Most fishing boats ran on noisy diesel engines you could hear from a mile away, especially the older workboats these guys would be familiar with. Modern speedboats could run quiet when they needed to.

I wanted to turn around and ask more questions, maybe buy the guy a beer and see what else he'd noticed. But that would blow my cover faster than a hurricane-force gust. Better to let the locals talk freely, let them think I was just another emergency worker grabbing lunch between boarding up windows. Sometimes the best intelligence came from just sitting quietly in the right place at the right time, letting people forget you were there.

Our burgers arrived, perfectly greasy and piled high with onions, lettuce, and tomatoes that looked like they'd been grown fresh on the island. Jimmy had a reputation for a reason —the meat was thick and juicy, the bun toasted just enough to hold together under the weight of toppings. I took a big bite, my mind already racing through the implications of what I'd heard. Were these operations new or established? Had someone been using this area as a route for months, or were they just now trying to take advantage of the hurricane chaos? Either way, it seemed someone wanted to try to shift product before the storm hit. I cursed myself for not pressing to send the team last night when the weather window was still open.

I'd need to alert the task force, increase surveillance if possible. But first, I needed more concrete evidence than bar talk and suspicious boat sightings. Hayes would want details, coordinates, something actionable.

"Probably just some rich idiots who don't know better," his companion said, dismissing the concern with a wave of his hand. "You know how them summer people are. Think they can ride out anything in their fancy boats."

"Ain't no yachts," the original speaker insisted, his voice carrying the authority of someone who knew the difference. "Too small, too fast. And running that tight formation? Nah, that's deliberate."

Tank nudged me with his elbow as Jimmy refilled our sweet tea glasses, the ice clinking against the sides. "Gonna be a rough one. Chief's got us all bunking at the station starting tonight."

My attention jerked toward my partner and my food, and I lost the thread of the other conversation for a moment as I forced myself to make appropriate small talk. Couldn't blow cover by looking too interested in what the locals were saying.

"Yeah, we'll be bunking there too. Chief McNamara cleared space in the rec room." I took another bite of my burger, letting the conversation flow naturally while straining to catch more from the two men down the bar. "Hope the generator holds up if we lose power."

Tank wolfed down the other half of his burger in two massive bites, barely pausing to chew. "Rec room's not bad. Got a TV, couple couches. Better than that time we had to sleep in the truck bay during that cat 4 that came through several years back."

I made appropriate noises of agreement while picking up the thread of conversation I'd been following earlier. The two men were discussing location now, and I focused hard to catch the details over the growing noise in the bar.

"—just north of that wreck, you know the one. Where Miller lost his boat last spring."

"That deep channel? Hell, even the local boys don't like running through there at night. Too many sandbars shift around after every storm."

"Exactly. Perfect spot if you don't want company." The first man's voice dropped lower, forcing me to lean slightly in his direction. "Saw them again this morning, same place. Definitely two boats this time."

His companion whistled low under his breath. "You tell anyone?"

"Who'm I gonna tell? Harbor patrol's too busy with storm prep. Coast Guard's got their hands full with evacuations. Besides, could be nothing."

But it wasn't nothing. I could feel it in my gut. Two boats running dark, using local knowledge of dangerous channels—it fit the pattern we'd been tracking up and down the coast. Smugglers often recruited local fishermen as pilots, using their expertise to navigate tricky waters that would ground or destroy Coast Guard cutters.

Tank's voice broke through my concentration like a foghorn. "You gonna finish those fries?"

I glanced down at the half-eaten pile of golden fries still sitting in the red plastic basket, completely forgotten while I'd been eavesdropping. "You know what? You take them. I'm gonna step outside and make a quick phone call."

As I slid off my stool, the door banged open, letting in a gust of wind that rattled the plywood we'd just spent the morning installing. More locals poured in, shaking rain from their hair and adding their voices to the growing chorus of concern about the approaching storm.

I slipped out of the bar and around the side of the building, finding a spot between a dumpster and a stack of crab traps where I'd be out of earshot of any eavesdroppers. The wind had picked up significantly, whipping my t-shirt against my chest and carrying the sharp scent of salt and approaching rain. Dark clouds were building on the horizon like an approaching army.

I pulled out my phone and put in a call to Commander Hayes. The signal was already getting weaker as the storm approached, and I had to cup my hand around the phone to hear clearly.

"Hayes." His voice crackled through the static, all business as usual.

"LaRue here, sir. Got something from Home Port bar. Two vessels reported running dark, using the deep channel through the shoals. Local spotted them last night and again this morning."

"Coordinates?"

"Not exact, sir. Based on the charts I studied and what these locals are describing, I can make an educated guess." I relayed the approximate position where I believed they were discussing, factoring in local landmarks and navigation hazards. "It's a tricky passage—lots of shifting sandbars, dangerous even for locals. Perfect spot if you're trying to avoid attention."

Hayes grunted his acknowledgment. "Matches our intelligence on previous patterns. Any visual confirmation?"

"Negative, sir. Just overheard two locals discussing it. One seemed like a credible witness—knew his waters well enough to spot something off. Talked like he'd been fishing these waters for decades."

"Noted. Keep your cover, LaRue. Focus on the storm prep mission we sent you there for. But..."

"Eyes and ears open. Yes, sir."

"And LaRue?" Hayes paused. "No heroics. You're there to gather intel, not to make arrests. Clear?"

"Crystal, sir."

I hung up and leaned against the weathered siding of the building, letting the salt air fill my lungs. Through the window, I could see Tank demolishing my abandoned fries with the same enthusiasm he'd shown for his burger. We still had six windows to board up, and the sky was darkening faster than I liked. The storm was coming whether we were ready or not.

Time to get back to work.

SEVEN

GABI

I paused in my chart notations as the radio shifted from music to the announcer.

"Good afternoon, Hatterwick Island. This is Sam Lewis coming to you live on WHAT with the latest on Hurricane Hannah. She has strengthened into an extremely dangerous Category 3 hurricane with winds of 115 mph as she works her way closer to our coast. According to the National Weather Service, additional strengthening is likely, so we may see winds up to 120 mph or more at landfall tomorrow evening."

It had been a while since we'd had a storm this strong. For about the fiftieth time today, I wished I weren't the only doctor on island. Of course, all our firefighters were certified EMTs, and there were a half-dozen nurses of varying skill levels—if we included the retirees. But I was extra cognizant that a lot of people were depending on me.

"I hope everyone has secured properties and finalized storm preparations. This is a life-threatening situation. As a reminder, the final ferry departing Hatterwick will leave from Sutter's Ferry in just under an hour at 3pm. After that, all ferries will be suspended. Emergency management has opened the high school gym and the community center for additional shelter capacity. For transportation, please call the emergency hotline number. I'll continue providing live radio updates as Category 3 Hurricane Hannah approaches. Stay safe, and remember we're all in this together, Hatterwick! Talk to you again soon."

The day had been a complete and utter shitshow from start to finish. Starting with this morning's evidence of an attempted break in, we'd rolled into a non-stop parade of patients with everything from minor cuts requiring stitches to more serious injuries that convinced me people lost all common sense when a hurricane was bearing down on us.

Throughout the entire chaotic day, I scrutinized every single person who came through the door, analyzing their behavior with the intensity of a detective to assess whether they might be casing the place for another attempt. I found myself watching for lingering glances toward the pharmaceutical storage area, noting who seemed overly interested in the layout of our facility, cataloging every nervous gesture or furtive look. But nobody paid any undue attention to the drug room or seemed to act particularly sketchy beyond the normal pre-storm jitters. Plenty of folks were jumpy and on edge, their movements quick and agitated, but given the hurricane rolling in with winds that could reach 120 mph, that level of anxiety wasn't at all surprising.

None of it made me feel any better about the security situation, though. The nagging worry sat in my stomach like a lead weight.

"Doc, you're up. Got a nasty sprained wrist in room two," Kristie announced, appearing in the doorway of the break room where I'd been trying to grab thirty seconds to down some lukewarm coffee. "Rads already pulled up for you."

Blowing out a long, exhausted breath, I added a few more

lines about my previous patient to the electronic chart notes, my fingers flying over the keyboard as I documented the treatment plan. Then I pushed back from the computer and stepped into room two, my sneakers squeaking on the linoleum floor.

Marion Zimmerman sat perched on the edge of the exam table, her legs dangling like a child's, cradling her left wrist close to her body in a protective gesture that told me she was in significant pain. Even from across the small room, I saw the angry purple and black bruising blooming across her joint, along with the obvious swelling of her wrist almost twice its normal size.

"Well now, Marion, what's happened to you?" I moved toward the sink to wash my hands.

"There was an unfortunate incident at the market over the last gallon of milk," she said with a rueful shake of her head, wincing as the movement jarred her injured wrist. "I got caught up in the crush when everyone made a mad dash for the dairy case. Went down hard when someone's cart clipped my legs."

I would never understand why people bought perishables like milk and eggs when the chances we'd lose power for days were almost a hundred percent. They'd have been so much better off stocking up on bottled water, canned goods, and protein bars—things that wouldn't spoil when the electricity went out. But it was a truth universally acknowledged among islanders that the milk, eggs, and toilet paper would always be the first items to disappear from the shelves whenever a storm threatened, as if these particular items possessed some magical hurricane-repelling properties.

"Dangerous place to be this close to a hurricane." I pulled on a fresh pair of latex gloves. "Half the island's probably crammed into those aisles right about now, grabbing whatever's left." I rolled the wheeled stool over to the exam table, positioning myself so I could get a better look at her injury.

"You're not wrong about that," Marion agreed with a bitter laugh. "It was like Black Friday in there, but with more panic and less organization. I even saw Willa and Sawyer trying to navigate through all the chaos."

At the mention of one of my oldest and dearest friends, my gaze flicked up from her swollen wrist to meet her eyes. "Oh, yeah? How were they holding up in all that madness?"

"Bless her heart, Willa looked a little green around the gills with all those people pressed in so close together." Sympathy colored Marion's voice. "You could tell she was struggling with the crowd."

Yeah, that was on-brand for Willa. She'd struggled with severe social anxiety all her life, ever since we were kids. Even back then, she'd always hung out on the fringes of crowds and social gatherings, despite the fact that she was basically island royalty as the latest generation of the founding Sutter family. Her discomfort in large groups had always been palpable, but that was always fine with me. As the youngest daughter of an absentee mother and a father with a reputation for being an abusive asshole, I hadn't exactly been cream of the social crop myself. But our differences in social standing had never mattered to either of us. We'd bonded over being outsiders in our own ways.

Marion continued talking as I gently began to palpate the injured area, though I hadn't done more than murmur a noncommittal "mmm-hmm," in response while I focused on my examination. "But Sawyer did such a good job shielding her from the worst of it, keeping people from bumping into her and creating a little buffer zone around her. I swear, watching those two together, they're absolute relationship goals."

Having somebody to stand by you no matter what? Hell

yeah, that was relationship goals. I could admit that left me feeling a little twinge of envy that one of my best friends had found it. And I had no patience for that twinge. I didn't begrudge her an iota of joy, and I was thrilled she'd finally gotten to marry the love of her life. It had no bearing on the fact that I was currently single. I'd find someone someday. It wasn't as if I were in the market right now. I still needed to process the dissolution of my last relationship. He'd put his career ahead of me. And you know what? That was fine. Right now, I was putting my career ahead of everything else. I'd worked my ass off to earn my medical degree so I could come back and serve the island that had always held my heart.

My exam backed up what Marion's x-rays had already told me. "Not broken, which is the good news. The bad news is you'll need to keep this immobilized for at least the next few days. We're going to put you in a splint. Over-the-counter anti-inflammatories for pain. Ideally, you'd ice it for fifteen or twenty minutes several times a day, but do the best you can, depending on what happens with the power. I'll send home a list of range of motion exercises for you to start in a few days, if the swelling has gone down. Under normal circumstances, I'd say come back in a week or two for a follow up, but who knows what we'll be dealing with after the storm. If you're not improving, come see us. Otherwise, it should heal just fine on its own, so long as you don't overtax it."

"Got it. Thanks, Doc."

"You stay safe, you hear?" I stepped out into the narrow hallway, the familiar antiseptic smell of the clinic mixing with the humid air that seemed to seep through every crack in the building. My phone had been vibrating against my hip for the past few minutes, and I finally fished it from my scrubs pocket. "Justin, can you get a wrist splint in here for Marion?"

"You got it," came his reply from somewhere down the hall, followed by the sound of cabinet doors opening and closing.

Glancing down at my phone screen, I saw my sister Caroline's name flashing across the display. She knew damn well I'd be slammed today, running around like a chicken with its head cut off, and Caroline wasn't the type to call over anything trivial. My stomach clenched as I swiped to answer. "Caro? What's wrong?"

"Why does anything have to be wrong?" Her voice carried that familiar note of forced lightness that meant she was definitely calling about something.

"Because my pregnant sister is calling me at work when we're less than twenty-four hours out from a Category 3 hurricane making landfall. So, forgive me for assuming this isn't a social call. What's going on?"

There was a pause, and I practically heard her organizing her thoughts. "I just wanted to know if you wanted me to go ahead and pack you a bag to take over to Hoyt's folks' house tomorrow? I know you left the house before dawn this morning, and I figured you're too slammed today to want to think about packing when you finally drag yourself home tonight."

I leaned against the wall, suddenly realizing this was yet another thing I could file under items I hadn't planned well enough. But then again, my plans had shifted dramatically since this morning, anyway. "No, actually. I'm going to be staying here at the clinic instead." The decision had been crystallizing in my mind all day, but saying it out loud made it feel more real, more final.

"The clinic?" Caroline's voice pitched higher with concern. "Gabi, is it even properly prepared for something like this? Will anyone be with you? I heard about that attempted break-in last night."

Of course she had. That was the Hatterwick Island

grapevine for you—news traveled faster than wildfire, especially when it involved anything remotely scandalous or dangerous.

"Caroline, I really don't have time to get into a whole discussion about this right now." Through the small window at the end of the hall, I could see the wind picking up, sending leaves and debris skittering across the parking lot. "I'm the only doctor on this entire island. I need to be somewhere I can access proper medical facilities if anything goes wrong during the storm."

Out of the corner of my eye, I spotted someone pushing through the front door, a bloody cloth wrapped around their hand, crimson already seeping through the makeshift bandage. My brain shifted back into full work mode. "And speaking of things going wrong, I've got another emergency walking through the door right now. I love you, and I'll see you when I make it home tonight. Just... be safe, okay?"

I ended the call before Caroline could launch into full big-sister mode and try to browbeat me into changing my plans. She'd have plenty of time to lecture me about my life choices after I got home.

Twenty minutes later, I had the deep gash on my patient's palm cleaned and stitched with eight precise sutures. In the distance, carried on the increasingly gusty wind, the deep, resonant boom of the ferry horn announced the final boarding call of the day. Two minutes to three o'clock. We were definitely getting down to the wire now. Unless more patients were expected or another emergency came stumbling through our doors, I needed to let my staff go finish battening down their own homes for the storm. And I needed to complete my own preparations for turning the clinic into my temporary hurricane shelter.

Escorting my last patient out to the front waiting area, I

opened my mouth to ask Nina about whether anyone else was on the schedule when I spotted a familiar figure standing near the reception desk. A tall, familiar figure in a Coast Guard uniform who had absolutely no business being anywhere near Hatterwick Island. A man who was supposed to be stationed on the other side of the damned country right now.

"What the hell are you doing here?" The words escaped before I could think better of them, but at least they came out cool and controlled rather than betraying the way my heart was hammering against my ribs.

Daniel tucked his hands deep into his pockets and slipped into that slow, laconic drawl that I both loved and hated in equal measure. "Well, at this particular moment, I'm here to help board up these windows and get this clinic ready to weather whatever Mother Nature's planning to throw at us. But if we're talking about the bigger picture, I'm on the Outer Banks for you, *cher*."

EIGHT

DANIEL

As I stared at the blank shock written across the face that had haunted my dreams for months, I was torn between a desire to freeze the moment to drink in every detail of her messy bun and the long-lashed, fathomless dark eyes locked on mine, and a deep regret for my big mouth. I hadn't meant to just come out with it like that—blurting out my feelings like some lovesick teenager in front of the entire damn clinic. No matter what kind of fantasies I'd harbored about her taking one look at me and leaping into my arms, I'd known the likelihood of that was slim to none. Not with how spectacularly I'd fucked up. But the moment I'd laid eyes on her, everything had just crystalized with startling clarity. All the careful speeches I'd rehearsed during the drive here had evaporated like morning mist.

Given that her expression didn't change—didn't soften, didn't warm, didn't show even a flicker of the affection that used to light up her features when she saw me—I knew I hadn't helped my cause. But damn, it was so good to see her. She looked good, with a trace of sun on those cheeks deepening her natural golden skin, telling me that no matter how hard she'd been working since she moved home to this island, she'd still found some outside time. Maybe early morning runs like she used to do back in Louisiana. Everything in me wanted to pull her into my arms and kiss the bejeezus out of her. To erase the distance I'd been fool enough to put between us with my stubborn pride and misplaced priorities. But I'd sure as shit lost the right to do that, so I didn't move.

Would this grand gesture I was making be enough? I'd changed my whole world to be here for her the way I should have in the first place. Requested a transfer, uprooted my entire life, burned bridges with my old station commander who'd made it clear he thought I was making a career-limiting mistake. But what if it was too late? What if she'd moved on? What if there was some old high school boyfriend she'd reconnected with since she came back to Hatterwick? Some local guy who understood island life in ways I never could? What if I'd potentially torpedoed my career and made this desperate move for nothing?

A host of what-ifs threatened to drown me, and more apologies rose on the tip of my tongue. But now was not the time nor the place. As the silence spun out well past the point of awkward and into downright uncomfortable territory, I realized everyone in the room was staring at me with varying degrees of confusion and curiosity. Because, yeah, I'd just made that announcement in front of her entire staff, the couple of patients sitting in the waiting room, and Tank.

Brilliant job, LaRue. Way to blow up your chances straight out of the gate.

Before Gabi said a word—before she told me to get the hell out or demanded an explanation—the door behind me opened with a sharp jingle of the bell.

"Oh, thank God. You're still here. We've got a problem."

Dragging my gaze away from Gabi's stunned face, I spotted a middle-aged woman supporting a guy whose face was pale with pain. A construction nail protruded through the top of his work boot, and blood was seeping through the leather.

Gabi hurried past me without so much as a glance, her training kicking in as she ducked under the guy's arm on the other side, helping stabilize him. "Mr. Dees, I really hope you're up to date on your tetanus shot." The professional mask slipped seamlessly into place, transforming her from the woman I'd loved and lost into Dr. Carrera. She snapped orders to her staff with crisp efficiency. "Justin, we're gonna put him in room one. Kristie, prep for extraction and disinfection."

I felt terrible for the poor guy with the nail in his foot, but I loved seeing Gabi work. She was competence personified, moving with practiced grace and unwavering confidence, and it was so very clear that this was what she was meant to do, where she was meant to do it. She'd told me that back in New Orleans, and I'd heard her, but I hadn't truly listened. I'd been too caught up in my own vision of success to understand that hers looked different.

Well, regret and I were becoming fast friends these days.

As all the medical staff disappeared to the back with their patient, I found myself left alone in the waiting area with a narrow-eyed woman I presumed was the office manager. Curiosity and suspicion warred in her pretty brown eyes as she sized me up. It was absolutely clear she wondered who the hell I was, what I was doing here, and why I'd just declared my love for her boss in front of half the island. She didn't trust me further than she could toss me, and honestly, I didn't blame her for that.

I respected a dragon guarding the gates.

"Right. We're here to board up the clinic's windows and

whatever else y'all need." I figured I should probably get back to the actual reason I was supposed to be here.

The woman—Nina, according to the nameplate on her desk—unfolded her arms and relaxed slightly. "Appreciate that. We've had back-to-back patients all day and haven't been able to get to it. There's plywood around back and a toolkit in the break room if you need anything extra."

Tank jerked a thumb toward the door. "We've got a drill and stuff in the truck. You just let us know what else y'all need. We'll get started on those windows."

"Thanks, hon. Y'all are lifesavers."

Recognizing a dismissal when I saw one, I followed Tank back outside into the humid air. The wind had picked up noticeably since our arrival, and dark clouds were building on the horizon. While he grabbed the tools from the truck, I circled around to the back of the building. Sure enough, several half sheets of plywood leaned against the pilings that elevated the structure. I hefted the first couple and moved around to the side where Tank waited, drill in hand.

He helped me lift the first piece of wood into position over a window, then let loose a low whistle as he positioned the drill. "I got no idea what's goin' on between you two, but I'm guessin' that did not go well."

I understood how small towns worked, and given my declaration in there was gonna be all over the island in a matter of days—I was granting a little extra time on account of the fact that folks were surely busy with the incoming storm—saying nothing wasn't an option. Better to control the narrative while I could.

"Nope. And that's all on me."

The big man leaned around me with the drill, starting the first screw. "It's a good thing Cap doesn't know anything about this."

Cap. Captain McNamaa, Gabi's brother-in-law. The man who'd probably want to feed me to the sharks if he knew I was here. The safest answer to that seemed to be a noncommittal grunt.

"What's the story with you and Gabi, anyway?"

There wasn't a chance in hell I was gonna tell this guy the full details before I could speak to her privately. But I could set the record straight on the generalities and start laying some groundwork for damage control. "We used to date, and I fucked it up. Made the wrong choice when it mattered. So I'm here to fix it."

"Huh." Tank processed this as we moved to the next window. "That takes some stones, I'll give you that."

We worked in silence for a few minutes, moving from one window to the next, the steady whir of the drill punctuating the growing wind. I tried not to think about what was happening inside, whether Gabi was talking about me, whether she was furious or hurt or just completely over it.

Unable to take it anymore. I looked over at Tank as he positioned another piece of plywood. "Is she dating somebody? Am I too late?"

"I haven't heard she's seein' anybody, but then again, Doc keeps her personal life pretty private. Mostly she's been working since she got back on-island, far as I know. She's been staying with Cap and her sister over at their house."

A flicker of hope lit in my chest at that. Maybe it wasn't too late. Maybe there was still a chance, assuming Tank was actually well-informed, which seemed a safe bet. Firehouses were usually hotbeds of gossip, and from what I could tell, this was a tight-knit community where everyone knew everyone else's business.

By the time the windows were covered, the last emergency —Mr. Dees—was hobbling out with his foot properly bandaged up and his wife fussing over him. Tank and I stepped inside to find things being shut down for the day.

"God willing, that's the last patient of the day." Gabi pulled off her latex gloves. "Let's shut it down. Y'all all need to get on home or wherever you're riding out the storm. Both of you have your emergency kits to take home?"

"Yep. All set and ready to go. There's one for you, too," Justin announced, holding up a medical bag.

"Thanks. But I'll have access to everything, as I'm riding out the storm here."

"Gabi, no! That's crazy talk." Nina's voice rose with concern. "This place isn't meant for riding out a hurricane."

"After this morning's incident with Mrs. Patterson, I feel it's necessary. And it's fine. The building's solid, and this way I'll be on-hand for any emergencies that arise during or after the storm."

"Are you even prepared for that with supplies?" Nina pressed. "Food, water, a place to sleep?"

"I'll get them sorted from home tonight and finish laying things in tomorrow after we set up the community center triage station."

So now I knew where she was going to be tomorrow. I filed that detail away, my mind already working on possibilities for damage control. I needed to find some way to approach her that didn't involve making a fool of myself in front of half the island.

"Now come on." Gabi began herding all of them toward the back exit. "Y'all go. Get home to your families. This is not up for debate."

"So we're good to go ahead and cover the front door?" Tank called out.

She sent me a long look over one shoulder, her dark eyes unreadable. For a moment, I thought she might say something —anything—but she just nodded. "Yes. We'll lock it behind you." Then she turned back to herding her staff toward the exit.

Okay. I can work with this. At least she wasn't telling me to get off the island. Yet.

Jerking my head toward the front, I followed Tank outside to put the last cover in place, my mind already racing with plans for tomorrow.

NINE

GABI

Once everyone was gone, I attacked the supply closet like it had personally offended me, counting packages of gauze and adhesive tape with military precision. The numbers went into my spreadsheet, each click of the keyboard another barrier between me and thoughts of Daniel.

Two hundred sterile gloves. Check.

IV bags. Check.

Antibiotics inventory. Check.

A memory of his voice saying he was here for me tried to surface. I slammed the cabinet shut and moved to the next task.

The clinic's generator needed testing. Again. I'd already checked it twice, but a third time wouldn't hurt. The steady hum as it kicked in provided blessed white noise, drowning out the echo of his words in my head.

My phone buzzed.

CAROLINE

Do you need help at the clinic?

And give her an uninterrupted opportunity to try to talk me out of staying? No, thank you.

GABI

I've got it handled. See you tonight.

The fewer people around right now, the better.

The equipment in each exam room needed securing. I wheeled the portable X-ray into the innermost room, farthest from the windows. The ultrasound followed. My checklist grew longer instead of shorter—each completed task spawning three more urgent needs.

Tomorrow we'd set up a triage station at the community center. I scribbled notes about supplies to transfer: basic first aid, splints, suture kits. I tried to focus on the list instead of memories of New Orleans. Of lazy Sunday mornings and plans Daniel and I had made together. Plans that implied we had a future. Of the moment he told me about the promotion that was already a done deal.

The pen pressed hard enough into the paper to leave impressions on the pages beneath.

My phone buzzed again. With a sigh, I pulled it from the pocket of my lab coat.

HOYT

Did the Coast Guard team finish boarding up the clinic windows?

GABI

They did.

HOYT

Need anything else?

GABI

No, I'm good.

HOYT

Sure?

GABI

Yes, Dad. 😄

I didn't mention that one of those Coast Guard members was my ex. My ex who was supposed to be in Seattle. Who was clearly *not* at the posting he'd thought so very fucking important three months ago.

My hand fisted around the pen I held. God, I wanted to call Willa. She'd know exactly what to say, how to untangle the mess of emotions churning in my stomach. Or maybe not. But she'd listen in that quiet, attentive way, and that would make me feel better. Probably.

But she and Sawyer were probably neck-deep in their own storm prep up at Sutter House on the north end of the island. Besides, what would I even tell her? That the man who chose Seattle over me suddenly decided to transfer to the Outer Banks? Had he transferred? Or was he somehow on loan for some weird reason? Hell, she didn't even know any of the details about Daniel to begin with, so I'd have to give backstory, and there was simply no time for that. Not that I wanted to relive that backstory to begin with. It was too painful.

The wind picked up outside, rattling the newly boarded windows. The storm was coming, whether my personal life was sorted out or not. My phone buzzed with a weather alert. Projected landfall in less than thirty hours. The time for personal drama had passed. And I was forced to admit that I'd done every damned thing that could be done to prepare the clinic for the storm. All the supplies were ready for transfer to the community center. There was nothing left to distract me here.

I didn't want to go home to my sister. She'd lay eyes on me

and know something was wrong, then she'd nag me in the most loving way possible until I spilled my guts about everything.

I wasn't ready to spill my guts. I wasn't sure I ever would be. There was a reason I hadn't told her about Daniel while we'd been together. Caroline and Hoyt were rock solid as a couple, and she believed everyone deserved the same. Deep down, so did I, but I knew not everyone was as lucky in finding their person as easily as the two of them had. She'd have had Opinions I didn't want to hear about the situationship. And given how things had turned out, she'd have probably been right. I didn't want to hear that either. Or her creative notions of punishment for his putting his job ahead of me, as well intentioned as they might be.

I thought about Bree. The Brewhouse might still be open. At least for the night. I could use a friend, and frankly, another drink. With that in mind, I stepped out of the clinic's back door, keys jingling as I locked up. I wished there'd been time to replace the lock, but nothing could be done about it now. I just had to hope that whoever had been by last night wouldn't try again.

The evening sun peeked through the building clouds, stretching my shadow long across the quiet employee parking lot. I took a half-dozen steps before something made the hair on my neck stand up. My fingers tightened around my keys. I scanned the area, searching for whatever had triggered my internal alarm.

A gull wheeled overhead. Out on the street, Mr. Mills walked his ancient golden retriever. A few cars rolled past. Nothing seemed out of place, but the sensation of being watched persisted. Maybe it was all the blank-faced buildings, their windows covered for the coming storm. It gave the whole area a sense of abandonment. Vaguely apocalyptic. As if zombies or raiders were prepared to leap out of the shadows at any moment.

Foolishness. You're just stressed over Daniel and what's coming.

I forced myself to breathe slow and steady. To think rationally. The lot was empty except for my car. Another sweep of the area revealed nothing suspicious, but my skin wouldn't stop crawling. I picked up my pace, clicking the key fob twice to unlock the doors. The beep seemed too loud in the quiet lot.

I slid behind the wheel and locked the doors immediately. Through the windshield, I kept watching, but still saw nothing concrete to justify this creeping unease. Only the wind beginning to whip the trees and the lengthening shadows of early evening. I'd get out of here and get that drink, and then I'd relax a bit.

The Brewhouse's neon signs were dark when I arrived, and I thought I was too late. But I spotted Bree's Jeep parked around back near the employee entrance. Gravel crunched under my tires as I pulled up next to it. The front door was still unlocked, and I ducked inside, grateful for the warm glow of the interior lights after the growing shadows outside.

The familiar scents of hops and wood polish enveloped me as I stepped into the main dining area. Bree glanced up from wiping down one of the high-top tables near the windows, clearly about to announce, "We're closed," but she took one look at my face and straightened, the cleaning rag forgotten in her hands. "You look like you've seen a ghost. What's wrong? You okay?"

"Just left the clinic." I rubbed my arms, trying to shake off the lingering unease that had followed me here. "Gave myself a serious case of the creeps walking through the empty building."

Understanding flickered across her features. "I heard about

the attempted break-in from Caroline when she stopped by earlier."

Of course she had. News traveled at light speed on Hatterwick, especially when it involved potential trouble.

Abandoning her cleaning rag on the table, Bree headed behind the polished oak bar. The distinct crack of a bottle cap being popped preceded her sliding a cold beer my way across the smooth surface. "We're mostly shut down until after the storm passes, but we've still got plenty of bottled stock. Sit for a bit and get your feet back under you. No sense rushing back out into that mess."

"Appreciate it more than you know." Now that I was here, surrounded by the warm familiarity of the Brewhouse, my case of the willies seemed completely stupid. But that paranoid feeling at the clinic wasn't why I'd come to begin with. I sank down into one of the cushioned chairs at a corner table and took a long pull on the bottle, letting the crisp beer settle my nerves. "So you know that situationship I mentioned yesterday?"

Bree's eyes sharpened with interest as she settled onto the stool beside me and propped her chin on her hand. "Yeah. What about him? Did something else happen?"

I took another long pull on my beer, buying myself a moment to figure out how to explain this disaster. "He's here."

Bree blinked, her eyebrows shooting up toward her hairline. "Here? On Hatterwick? Right now? Why the hell would he be here?"

"Coast Guard hurricane preparation and emergency response." I began to pick at the damp label on my bottle, peeling off small strips. "And apparently..." The words stuck in my throat for a moment. "He claims he's here for me."

She leaned forward on her elbows, her expression shifting from surprise to something approaching outrage. "Tell me everything. Start from the beginning and don't leave anything out."

So I did. As briefly as possible while still hitting the important points, I explained Seattle. The job offer that had seemed like everything he'd ever wanted. The promotion that had come with a cross-country move. The way he'd made his choice without consulting me, then seemed genuinely shocked when I couldn't just pick up and follow him across the country. The end of things that had felt more like a whimper than the dramatic conclusion our relationship probably deserved.

By the time I finished, her face had darkened considerably, a storm brewing in her eyes that rivaled the one heading our way. "The absolute audacity of that man! He chose Seattle over you. He chose his career advancement over your relationship. He doesn't get to just show up months later, in the middle of a hurricane no less, and claim he's here for you like some kind of romantic gesture."

Her instant feminine outrage was exactly what I needed. Some of the disquiet that had been churning in my stomach since Daniel's unexpected appearance finally settled. "That's exactly what I thought when he cornered me at the clinic." I traced random patterns in the condensation gathering on my bottle. "I'm just going to ignore him until the storm passes and he gets reassigned somewhere else."

"On this tiny island?" Bree snorted, shaking her head. "During a hurricane evacuation and emergency response? Good luck with that plan, girl."

I shrugged, trying for nonchalance I didn't feel. "It's going to be complete chaos. Everyone running around preparing for landfall, setting up the community center as a shelter, coordinating storm response teams. How hard can it really be to avoid one Coast Guard petty officer?"

"Gabi." Her raised eyebrows suggested I was being deliberately obtuse. "You're the only doctor on this island. He's Coast Guard emergency response. You really think there's any universe where you won't end up working together before all this is over?"

The truth of that statement hit me like an icy wave. Of course we'd end up working together. Medical emergencies didn't pause for personal drama, and hurricane response required all hands on deck. "I think we're both going to be too damned busy dealing with the immediate aftermath of this storm to worry about anything else." Not that I was actively wishing disaster on my island, but facts were facts.

Bree pushed back from the table and crossed back to the bar, grabbing a beer for herself. "Look, I get it. The last thing you want is to deal with relationship drama when you're trying to save lives and keep people safe. But you can't just keep avoiding him indefinitely."

I gave her the side eye, raising an eyebrow pointedly. "I don't know about that. You've been doing a pretty admirable job avoiding Ford for the past decade or so."

She had the grace to wince at that observation. "Touché. But the fact that he's been deployed on the other side of the world for most of that time definitely helps with the avoidance strategy." She took a sip of her beer before continuing. "I'm just saying, it seems like you're gonna have to face him, eventually. If for no other reason than to get a little bit of closure on whatever you two had. A guy doesn't show up making grand declarations like 'I'm here for you' and then let a little thing like a Category 3 hurricane get in his way. Even if he has to wait until cleanup and recovery operations are finished, I somehow doubt he's going to just quietly leave the island without at least trying to talk to you again."

The thought of having that conversation—really talking through what had happened between us, what had gone wrong, whether there was anything salvageable—made my stomach clench with anxiety. Could I handle a civil conversation to get some kind of closure on our relationship? Could I trust myself not to either completely fall apart or say something I'd regret?

Honestly, I had no idea.

"I really like my avoidance plan better," I said, taking another long drink.

Bree arched a brow and smirked, the expression highlighting the mischievous streak I'd always admired in her. "Good luck with that, Dr. Carrera."

TEN

DANIEL

I hefted another box of emergency supplies onto the stack, my shoulders protesting the movement with a sharp twinge that shot down my spine. The ibuprofen I took at dawn hadn't even begun to touch the deep, grinding ache from hours of holding binoculars steady in the pre-dawn darkness. My neck felt like someone had taken a crowbar to it, and every muscle in my back screamed in protest as I straightened up.

"These the last of them?" Martinez passed me another box from the truck, sweat already beading on his forehead despite the cooler morning air.

"Two more." I blinked hard against the grit in my eyes, feeling like someone had poured sand under my eyelids. The coffee maker in the fire station's kitchen had been working overtime since 5am, churning out cup after cup of thick, bitter brew, but caffeine could only do so much against bone-deep exhaustion and the weight of frustration settling in my chest.

My night watching Miller's wreck was a complete and total bust. No boats, no lights, no suspicious activity—just choppy water and increasing wind that made every shadow into a potential threat. The storm's outer bands were already hitting the coast, creating white-capped waves that made it impossible to spot anything smaller than a cruise ship without proper equipment. Either there'd been nothing out there to begin with, or we'd already missed our window by hours, possibly days.

"You look like hammered shit." Tank dropped a case of water bottles at my feet with a solid thunk, his massive frame blocking out what little sunlight filtered through the gathering clouds. "Thought you turned in early last night."

I grunted, not bothering with an answer as I hefted the water case and added it to the growing pile. The less said about my unauthorized surveillance operation, the better. Commander Hayes would have my ass in a sling if he knew I'd gone out alone without backup or proper gear, crouched behind that jetty like some kind of amateur detective. But something about those fishermen's story kept nagging at me all day yesterday, demanding investigation even when logic told me to let it go.

"Last one." Martinez handed over the final box, this one heavier than the rest and marked with red tape indicating medical supplies. "Better get this stuff distributed before the wind picks up more. Chief Thompson wants everything battened down by noon."

The mid-morning radio briefing put the hurricane just nine hours out from making landfall. Already the sky stretched out that strange, sickly greenish that preceded major storms, the kind of color that made your skin crawl and your teeth ache. The air was heavy and electric, charged with an energy that made the hair on my arms stand up. My joints ached with the pressure change—or maybe that was just from spending four hours crouched behind a jetty with nothing to show for it but a crick in my neck and the bitter taste of failure.

The wind gusted suddenly, rattling the fire station's storm

shutters with a metallic clatter that echoed through the bay. I'd wasted precious hours chasing shadows while the storm bore down on us like a freight train. Now I needed to focus on what I was actually here for—helping Hatterwick weather whatever was coming, not playing detective with half-baked theories and gut instincts.

I paused in the doorway of the station's office, catching fragments of conversation between Chief Thompson and Captain McNamara. The chief's voice carried the weight of decades of experience, steady and authoritative even under pressure.

"... need the community center prepped by fourteen hundred hours." Chief Thompson's voice carried down the hall, punctuated by the rustle of papers and the occasional squeak of his chair. "Got word from the clinic about setting up triage—Dr. Carrera's got specific requirements for the medical station."

"Already on it." McNamara's response was clipped, focused, the kind of tone that came from years of emergency response training. "But we're short on manpower. Half the crew's out securing the marina, and the other half's dealing with evacuation orders."

I shifted my weight from one foot to the other, joints protesting. The mention of the clinic caught my attention immediately. Gabi had talked about emergency protocols yesterday while we'd finished up with the windows.

"What's the timeline looking like?" I heard Thompson tapping his pen against the desk in a steady rhythm.

"Three or four hours tops before conditions start to deteriorate seriously. Need to get those beds set up, oxygen tanks secured and properly anchored. Gabi's got a whole checklist—color-coded, cross-referenced, the works. Woman's more organized than a military operation."

I stepped into the office, clearing my throat to announce my presence. "Need an extra set of hands?"

Both men turned toward me, Chief Thompson's weathered face creasing in what might have been relief. McNamara's expression remained neutral, professional, but something flickered in his eyes—recognition, maybe. Or suspicion. Hard to tell with a guy who kept his cards close to his chest.

Did Tank say something about my prior involvement with Gabi? I hadn't given him much in the way of details during our brief conversation yesterday, but I'd said enough to potentially put her brother-in-law on the defensive. The last thing I needed was family drama complicating an already tense situation.

After a beat that stretched just long enough to be uncomfortable, he acknowledged, "Could use the help."

"Happy to pitch in wherever needed." I kept my voice steady, professional, even as my mind automatically catalogued the quickest routes to the clinic from here.

The fire chief nodded approvingly. "Appreciate the assist, LaRue. Hoyt, get him up to speed on the layout and what still needs doing."

I followed McNamara into the hall, my boots echoing against the polished concrete floor, ignoring the voice in my head pointing out that this was a thin excuse to put myself in Gabi's path again. The community center needed the help— that was reason enough. At least that's what I told myself as we gathered supplies and headed out into the increasingly hostile weather.

It took less than a quarter hour to mobilize a group to help, but every minute felt precious as the wind continued to pick up and the sky darkened overhead.

The community center's double doors banged against the wall with a sharp crack as Tank shouldered them open, his massive arms full of medical supplies that would have taken two normal people to carry. I followed close behind with my own load, immediately hit by the smell of disinfectant that was already heavy in the air, mixing with the scent of fresh tarp and the faint mustiness of the old building.

Inside, the basketball court looked like a scene from a disaster movie. Blue tarps covered the polished wooden floor in neat sections, dividing up emergency shelter from medical space. A group of volunteers wheeled in IV poles while others assembled privacy screens, their movements coordinated despite the underlying tension of impending crisis. The familiar sounds of a gymnasium—squeaking shoes, echoing voices—had been replaced by the efficient bustle of emergency preparation.

"Over here." McNamara directed us toward a staging area where other firefighters sorted supplies into clearly labeled zones—trauma, respiratory, cardiac, each marked with different colored tape for quick identification. The organization impressed me—whoever had planned this layout knew their stuff and had clearly thought through every possible scenario.

"Those go in bay three." A nurse I recognized from yesterday pointed to our boxes, her scrubs already damp with sweat as she juggled multiple clipboards and directed the constant flow of volunteers. "And we need more hands setting up the isolation area in the back corner—Dr. Carrera was very specific about the ventilation requirements."

I stacked the supplies where indicated, my movements automatic while my eyes swept the room, searching for any sign of Gabi's familiar figure. Surely, she was here somewhere, overseeing all this preparation. This level of organization, the attention to detail—it had her fingerprints all over it.

Then I joined Tank in wrestling cots into position, the work methodical but physically demanding. Each cot needed to be precisely placed according to the tape markings on the floor, with exact spacing for equipment access and patient privacy.

Tank worked with a surprising delicacy for such a big man, his massive hands carefully adjusting the positioning with millimeter precision.

"You expecting someone?" Tank grunted as we locked another cot's legs in place, sweat dripping from his forehead despite the air conditioning.

"Just trying to get a headcount." The lie came easy, too easy, sliding off my tongue without conscious thought.

The side eye Tank shot me said he wasn't buying what I was selling, not even a little bit. His expression was knowing, almost amused, like he'd seen this particular dance before.

The clinic office manager—Nina, I remembered from yesterday's introductions—directed us to move supplies from the staging area to the medical station setup. As we worked, lifting boxes and arranging equipment, I caught fragments of conversation floating through the organized chaos—supply counts, staff assignments, patient capacity estimates. Every voice carried an undercurrent of controlled urgency.

"Where's Dr. Carrera?" Another nurse called across the room, her voice cutting through the general noise. "These medication protocols need sign-off before we can finish the pharmacy setup."

Nina glanced up from her seemingly endless checklist, pen poised in midair. "Still at the clinic. She's still seeing patients on an emergency basis, trying to clear as many cases as possible before we have to shut down regular operations."

My hands tightened involuntarily on the box I was carrying, knuckles going white as my mind immediately shifted gears. The timeline in my head had seemed manageable when we started—three hours had seemed like plenty of time. Now, with the darkening sky visible through the high windows and the strengthening winds audible even inside the building, that buffer was evaporating fast.

I should stay here. I knew that. The community center needed every available hand, and I had my orders from Commander Hayes. But my mind kept circling back to our last real conversation, the look on Gabi's face when I'd told her why I was really here on the island. The way she'd disappeared into her work afterward without another word, professional distance replacing the easy warmth we'd shared.

"LaRue!" McNamara's voice cut through my thoughts like a blade. "Need those supplies over at station four."

I forced myself to focus on the immediate task, carrying boxes and setting up equipment even as part of my brain calculated distances and drive times. How long would it take to reach the clinic from here? How much time did we actually have before the roads became impassable? Whether I had any right to go after her at all, given how things had been left between us.

The wind howled against the building's metal roof with increasing intensity, and the emergency lights flickered once, twice—a warning of things to come. Through the windows, I could see palmetto trees bending at impossible angles, their fronds whipping through the air like green flags of surrender.

The radio at my hip crackled to life with a burst of static. "LaRue, come in."

I fumbled for the device, nearly dropping the medical supplies I'd been sorting. "Go ahead."

"It's Rawlings." The voice was tight with stress, competing with wind noise in the background. "Need you at the marina ASAP. Got multiple vessels breaking loose from their moorings —it's turning into a real shitshow down here."

Damn it. I glanced toward the community center's entrance, still hoping against hope that Gabi might appear through those doors. The past hour had crawled by with no sign of her, despite my constant scanning of every new arrival.

"Copy that. On my way."

Tank clapped me on the shoulder with one of his massive hands, the gesture somehow both reassuring and dismissive. "I got this covered here. Go do what you gotta do."

I jogged through the strengthening wind toward the loaner truck from the fire department, feeling the weather trying to knock me sideways with each gust. The sky had turned an ugly shade of green-black that reminded me of old bruises, and the air felt thick enough to chew. My hands clenched the steering wheel as I navigated the nearly empty streets, debris already starting to accumulate in the gutters.

The clinic's lights glowed like a beacon in the growing darkness as I passed, warm yellow squares cutting through the gloom. The angle was wrong for me to see past the landscaping to the employee lot at the back where Gabi would be parked. I fought the overwhelming urge to pull over, to just take two minutes to make sure she was there and safe. But people's lives and livelihoods were literally at stake at the marina—boats worth hundreds of thousands of dollars breaking free to smash into docks and other vessels. I couldn't justify a detour for personal reasons, no matter how much every instinct screamed at me to check on her. Besides, where else would she be? She'd said yesterday she intended to ride out the storm at the clinic, and Dr. Gabriella Carrera always did exactly what she said she would do.

The radio squawked again, urgent static preceding the voice. "LaRue, what's your ETA? We're losing boats faster than we can secure them."

"Two minutes out." I pressed the accelerator harder, the truck's engine straining against the headwind as I left the clinic's comforting lights behind in my rearview mirror. The wind buffeted the vehicle like invisible hands trying to push me off course, and debris skittered across the road in deadly patterns—

palm fronds, pieces of siding, things I couldn't identify in the growing darkness.

I had to trust she knew what she was doing. That she had an evacuation plan if everything went south. That someone else was looking out for her safety while I dealt with my own responsibilities. Dr. Carrera was nothing if not prepared, organized, and competent. She didn't need me riding to her rescue like some kind of knight in Coast Guard fatigues.

But as I turned toward the marina, tires fighting for traction on the increasingly slick road, all I could think about was how I'd failed to look out for her before. How I'd let my career advancement pull me away from her without even discussing it, without giving her a chance to weigh in on decisions that affected both of us. And now here I was again, driving in the opposite direction when every fiber of my being screamed at me to turn around, to make sure she was safe before worrying about anyone or anything else.

The marina came into view through the windshield, and I could see the chaos even from a distance—boats tilting at crazy angles, lines snapping in the wind, people running between the docks in what looked like barely controlled panic. My duty was clear, my training kicking in automatically. But my heart remained stubbornly focused on a small clinic growing smaller in my mirrors, and the woman I'd never stopped loving who was still there, still working, still putting everyone else's needs before her own safety.

ELEVEN

GABI

"Hey Hatterwick, Sam Lewis here, broadcasting live on WHAT as we start to see the first effects of Hurricane Hannah. The storm's massive outer bands are reaching us now, bringing driving rain, powerful wind gusts, and rising seas. I hope everyone has finished preparations and reached safe shelter."

"Working on it," I muttered.

In my haste to get out the door this morning before Caroline could attempt an interrogation, I'd forgotten my bag. The clinic itself was ready, but I didn't have my personal supplies, so as soon as I'd gotten the last patient on their way, I'd hustled back across the island to the house to grab my bag, along with some additional supplies to see me through my long night at the clinic. I spent far too long on that, cursing myself for my lack of forethought when the rain kicked up in earnest as I was loading my car. But I'd been pitifully grateful that Caroline and the kids were already at her in-laws' because I was already too damned tired to hide my emotional turmoil from her. Considering I never actually told her about Daniel in the first place, that was a conversation I wasn't particularly interested in having.

Daniel, who claimed to have come to the Outer Banks for me.

Nope. Not going there. Not yet.

I'd kept myself busy enough with last-minute patients that I'd been able to hold most thoughts of him at bay today. The steady stream of worried islanders needing prescriptions refilled, minor injuries treated, and reassurances given had provided the perfect distraction from the chaos he'd stirred up in my chest. But I wouldn't have that luxury during the storm. The long, quiet hours stretching ahead would leave me with nothing but time to think, to dissect every word he'd said, every look that had passed between us. I'd have to deal with the complicated swirl of emotions he'd kicked up eventually, but I needed to get back to the clinic first. I needed the familiar comfort of my workspace, my sanctuary, before I could even begin to untangle this mess.

"According to the latest from the National Weather Service, conditions will rapidly deteriorate in the next 60 minutes as the Category 3 hurricane's core draws closer with its 120-mile-per-hour winds. We can expect widespread power outages, downed trees and power lines, severe flooding in coastal areas, and potentially significant structural damage across the island as Hannah unleashes her full fury. This will be a long night, folks."

I hoped like hell I made it back to the clinic before the power went down. The last thing I needed was to be fumbling around in the dark, trying to navigate flooded streets by the glow of my headlights. I'd done a fantastic job prepping the medical side of things—emergency supplies organized, backup power systems tested, critical medications secured—but my impulsive decision to ride the storm out here had led to a half-assed preparation at best for myself. One of the big delays had been hunting down the battery-powered camp lantern buried somewhere in Caroline's closet and scrounging up some candles from various drawers around the house, so at least I wouldn't be spending the whole night in the unrelieved dark. The thought of sitting alone in that clinic, listening to Hannah tear the island apart while surrounded by pitch blackness, made my skin crawl.

I had a generator, but I wouldn't waste it until the storm was past, in case utilities were knocked out for longer than a day or two. The diesel fuel was precious, and there was no telling when the next supply boat would make it to the island. The medications requiring refrigeration were covered by a smaller battery unit that would keep them cool for the next twenty-four hours. Then we'd see what there was to see. I'd done everything I could think of, but the nagging sense that I'd forgotten something important gnawed at me.

"Emergency responders are standing by to mobilize once the worst of the storm passes. In the meantime, hunker down and stay away from windows. Don't go outside for any reason until well after the storm has left the area. I'll continue broadcasting storm coverage and updates from the WHAT emergency studio. Stay safe, Hatterwick. We'll get through this together!"

The empty streets of the village and the boarded-over houses, was like being on the set of some apocalypse movie. The familiar shops and restaurants I passed daily looked alien and forbidding behind their plywood shields. Not a soul was out, which was exactly as it should be. Even the seagulls had vanished, driven inland or to whatever shelter they could find. The only movement came from debris already starting to skitter across the asphalt and the occasional loose piece of plywood flapping ominously in the wind.

When the clinic came back into view, I exhaled a sigh of relief that was short-lived. At least until I wheeled into the lot and spotted the figure tucked under the overhang of the back door, hunched inside a dark rain slicker like some kind of storm-battered refugee.

My hands tightened on the wheel until my knuckles went white. Had the prospective thief already come back? Had someone decided to take advantage of the storm to break into the clinic? My heart hammered against my ribs as adrenaline flooded my system.

Then he turned to face me, and the glare of headlights illuminated his face through the driving rain.

Daniel.

The sight of him punched me in the gut like a physical blow, stealing my breath and making my vision swim for a moment. Again. Just when I thought I'd gotten my equilibrium back, there he was, disrupting everything with his mere presence.

I hadn't allowed myself to think about him or his ludicrous declaration. I'd been too busy trying to deal with the endless stream of patients, focusing on their needs instead of the turmoil churning in my chest. And now here he was again, like some kind of stubborn ghost I couldn't shake. Bags of some kind clustered around his feet, as if he'd been camping out there for who knew how long.

This was the last thing I needed with the storm bearing down, with my nerves already stretched thin from the day's preparations and the looming night ahead.

I'm in the Outer Banks for you, cher.

His words echoed through my head, bouncing around like pinballs and refusing to settle anywhere that made sense. Each repetition was another small explosion going off in my chest.

What the fuck did that even mean? This jackass had

broken my heart into so many pieces I'd thought I'd never find them all. He'd chosen his career over me without hesitation or discussion, decided for both of us like my feelings didn't matter at all. Did he think he could just show up and sweep me away after all this time? That I'd abandon the job and all the work I'd put in to prove myself worthy of the trust this community had placed in me? Because fuck that shit. If he believed I'd do that, if he thought I'd follow him anywhere, it just proved yet again that he didn't know me at all to begin with. That maybe he never had.

Fueled by fresh temper that burned hot and bright in my chest, I parked as close to the building as possible and tugged up the hood of my raincoat. The wind immediately tried to rip it back down, and rain stung my face like needles. I didn't even speak to him as I got out of the car, deliberately avoiding eye contact while snagging my duffel bag of supplies from the passenger seat. The weight of his gaze was a physical thing, heavy and expectant, but I refused to acknowledge it.

He stepped aside as I climbed the steps and approached the door, water streaming off both of us onto the concrete. I tried not to notice how the rain plastered his dark hair to his head, how it made his eyes look even more startlingly blue against his tanned skin. I tried not to remember how it felt to run my fingers through that hair, how those eyes used to look at me like I was his whole world.

When I got the door open, he just marched right in behind me, uninvited, bringing the smell of rain and something distinctly him that made my chest tighten with unwanted recognition.

"What the hell are you doing?" The words came out sharp with all the frustration and hurt I was trying so hard to contain. Other than dripping all over my floors and making himself at home in my space without permission. How long had he been standing out there, getting soaked to the bone? I shut down the momentary twinge of sympathy before it could take root. I hadn't invited him here. I didn't owe him concern or care.

"Bringing in supplies." He hefted the bags he'd dragged in with him, his voice matter-of-fact as if this was the most natural thing in the world. "If you're gonna ride things out, you're gonna need stuff."

I dropped my own bag to the floor of the break room with more force than necessary, the thud echoing in the small space. The break room was the innermost windowless room of the building, the safest place to hunker down when Hannah hit with full force. "I brought my own."

"Doesn't hurt to have more." He set his own bags down with more care, and I caught glimpses of what looked like emergency rations, bottled water, and other supplies spilling out.

"Do you not have work to do somewhere else?" I stripped off my rain jacket and hung it on the hook by the door, trying to inject as much dismissal into my voice as possible. "Shouldn't you be out there being all heroic and Coast Guard-y?"

"We're done with work for now. Things are battened down, and my men are riding out the storm at the firehouse."

"Then why aren't you with them?" I turned to face him fully for the first time since he'd appeared like some kind of unwanted apparition. "Shouldn't you be with your team?"

"Because I'm not leaving you here to ride this out by yourself. It's not safe."

The presumption in his voice, the casual way he said it like it was his decision to make, sent fury racing through my veins. "In case you've forgotten, you abdicated the right to take care of me, LaRue. You gave that up when you chose Seattle over me. And I'm perfectly capable of handling the storm on my own."

"Sure you are." His eyes tracked over me with an intensity that made my skin prickle with awareness. "You're one of the most capable people I've ever met. It's sexy as hell. I'm still not leavin' you by yourself."

The swirl of emotion rose so fast it all but choked me, a tsunami that threatened to drag me under. So much rage—at him for what he'd done, for the casual way he'd shattered my world and walked away. For being here when I'd just started to put the end of us behind me, when I'd finally begun to build something that was mine alone. And at myself for being even a little bit relieved at the idea of not being here alone, for the treacherous part of my heart that still responded to his presence despite everything.

Why the hell did it have to be *him?* Of all the people who could have shown up to keep me company during the storm, it had to be the one person I'd spent months trying to forget. The one who knew exactly how to get under my skin, how to make me feel things I didn't want to feel.

"You weren't invited." The words came out flat and cold, each one carefully measured.

"I can stay out of your way. I'm just here to help."

"Just here to help. Just our friendly neighborhood Coast Guardsman." Sarcasm dripped from every syllable like venom. "Except this isn't your neighborhood. You're supposed to be in Seattle, living your dream life. And I'm not feeling remotely friendly toward you."

"That's totally fair, *cher*," he said easily, and the familiar endearment hit me like a slap. The casual way he said it, like nothing had changed, like he still had the right to call me that.

It *was* totally fair. I had every right to be angry, every right to want him gone. So why the hell did the notion of him validating my feelings make me even more furious? Why did his easy acceptance of my anger seem like another kind of dismissal?

As if my emotional storm had conjured it, wind and rain

crashed against the building like a physical assault, the sound so violent it made me flinch. The storm had fully hit with the fury the weather service had promised, and my window to evict him had slammed shut as decisively as the hurricane shutters over the clinic's windows. For better or worse, I was stuck with my ex for the next several hours, trapped in this small space while Hannah raged outside.

The irony wasn't lost on me. I'd been dreading spending the night alone, and now I had company. Just not the kind I would have chosen in a million years.

Well, shit.

TWELVE

DANIEL

Wind and rain battered the clinic building with relentless fury, each gust sending tremors through the walls that I felt in my bones. But even the raw power of Mother Nature was nothing compared to the chill anger radiating from Gabi like arctic air from an open freezer. She was a woman of great passion in all things—her work, her family, her convictions, her love. It was something I'd always appreciated about her, something that had drawn me to her like a moth to flame from the very beginning. If I'd just pissed her off in some ordinary way, she'd have let me know in no uncertain terms, probably with a few choice words in both English and Spanish that would've peeled the paint off the walls.

In a heartbeat, I'd have taken the blistering heat of her Latina temper over this cool indifference that felt like being slowly frozen to death.

She sat at a table across the room, her back ramrod straight, stubbornly not looking in my direction or otherwise acknowledging my presence in any meaningful way. That alone let me know exactly how badly I'd fucked things up. The silence between us had weight and substance, pressing down on the room like a physical force. She hadn't said a word for the past three hours—not since we'd more or less made nests for ourselves on opposite sides of the break room, which was the center-most, windowless space in the building and our best bet for riding out whatever hell Hannah had in store for us.

We'd grabbed mattresses from a couple of the patient beds and brought them in to lie on, if we ever actually tried to sleep. Mine was positioned near the door, hers closer to the far wall, with what felt like an ocean of charged silence stretching between us. The fluorescent lights overhead buzzed and flickered intermittently as the wind outside howled like something alive and angry.

I'd been racking my brain for the better part of those three hours, trying to think of something—anything—to break the ice between us. Sure, an apology was right up there at the top of my mental list, but just blurting it out didn't seem like it would get me far. I needed to build up to that, create some kind of opening so I was sure she at least heard me, even if she didn't believe a single word coming out of my mouth.

The problem was, I'd never been good with words when it mattered most. Give me a tactical situation, a rescue operation, a crisis on the water—I could handle all of that without breaking a sweat. But this? Trying to find my way back to the one person who'd ever really mattered? I was floundering worse than a greenhorn in his first storm.

So far, the power had held, but I knew it was only a matter of time before the lines snapped under the assault of wind and debris, and we were plunged into the twilight world of lanterns and candles. The building groaned around us, a constant reminder of the hurricane's growing strength. I could break out the supplies I'd brought and try to feed her. Given how busy she'd been moving between patients, checking charts, coordinating with her small staff, I suspected she hadn't eaten in hours.

That had often happened during her residency in New Orleans. She got so caught up in her work, so focused on taking care of everyone else, that she forgot to take care of herself. Back then, bringing her a meal had often been the only time we got to spend together during her grueling schedule, and I'd always taken great pleasure in feeding her. Watching her face light up when I'd show up with her favorite po' boy or a container of my grandmother's gumbo. Those had been some of the best moments we'd shared.

From across the room, cutting through the storm's noise and the tension between us, her belly growled loudly enough that I heard it.

Okay, Universe, message received.

I grabbed one of the waterproof bags I'd kept stowed on the Zodiac and began unpacking the contents, hoping the rustling might draw her attention without seeming too obvious about it. Cured meats, various cheeses, water crackers, applesauce pouches, dried fruit, tortilla chips, and salsa. It had started out part charcuterie board in my mind and ended up part camping fare as I'd grabbed whatever nonperishables were in my quarters at Nag's Head.

The salsa would definitely be below her standards—she made a hell of a homemade one with fresh tomatoes and peppers that brought tears to your eyes in the best possible way —but either way, it wasn't a bad spread for hurricane rations. Again, she said nothing as I opened containers and began loading a paper plate, but I caught her stealing glances in my direction when she thought I wasn't looking.

Maybe she was still avoiding even looking at me directly, but at least I had her attention.

When I crossed over and thrust the plate toward her, she

looked up with a frown that could've curdled milk. "What is this?"

"Food. I'm guessin' you haven't eaten in hours." I kept my voice carefully neutral, not wanting to sound like I was lecturing her or trying to take care of her when she clearly didn't want my care.

Her gaze strayed to the nearby bag, where I spotted some protein bars sticking out of a side pocket—clearly her own emergency provisions.

I shimmied the plate a little, offering a small smile. "It's not boudin balls, but it's gonna be better than that cardboard you've got over there."

Her eyes snapped to mine at the reminder of one of her favorite dishes from my kitchen. For a moment, something flickered in those dark eyes, a crack in the ice wall she'd built between us. I thought for a moment she'd turn the food down out of sheer spite, but at last she accepted the plate with reluctant fingers.

"Thank you." The words were stiff, formal, but they were something.

"No problem." I returned to the table to build my own plate, trying to act casual, though my heart was hammering against my ribs. "I'm surprised you didn't have a more elaborate setup yourself. As I recall, you absolutely know how to throw a hurricane party. Even if it's just for one."

I glanced back in time to see her shoulders hunch, and I knew I'd stepped on something tender.

"I'd originally intended to ride out the storm with my sister and her kids over at her in-laws' house." Her voice was carefully controlled, but I heard the hurt underneath.

"Why didn't you? I mean, I know Hoyt had to work." The words were out before I could stop them, and I immediately regretted bringing up her brother-in-law.

That earned me another sharp look, this one with an edge of suspicion.

"I've been liaising with the fire department since I got here," I explained quickly. "Met him yesterday morning. Seemed like a good guy." Which was true—Hoyt McNamara had struck me as exactly the kind of solid, dependable man you'd want watching over your family.

"Ah." She popped a dried apricot into her mouth, chewing thoughtfully. "I changed my mind because there was an attempted break-in at the clinic yesterday."

I remembered the scratches on the back door—fresh gouges in the metal that looked like someone had been working at it with a crowbar or something similar. "Somebody tried to jimmy the back door?"

Her tone dropped another few degrees, becoming almost arctic. "Did my staff get chatty?"

"Nope. Noticed it while I was waiting on you to get back." I took a bite of cheese and crackers, trying to keep things casual, even though my mind was already running through possibilities, none of them good.

She hummed a noncommittal note, the sound barely audible over the storm.

"There been any previous break-ins?" I pressed gently.

"Not since I've been here. And neither Dr. Sibley nor anyone else on the staff has mentioned it. Plus, if someone had tried before, it would have gotten all over the island, and my sister would've told me." She gestured vaguely with a cracker. "You know how small towns work."

Not a regular target then, which made it more concerning, not less.

"So you decided to ride the storm out by yourself, in case they came back?" I prompted, trying to keep the worry out of my voice.

"Partly." She was being deliberately evasive, and it was driving me crazy.

"What exactly are you planning on doing if somebody does come back?" I tried to keep the judgment out of my tone, but I didn't at all like the idea that some kind of tweaker might be hanging around, looking for easy drugs to steal. Or worse, that some of the traffickers we'd been tracking might've decided to target the clinic for an easy score during the chaos of the storm. It wasn't their usual MO, but we weren't dealing with the cream of society here. Crimes of opportunity were a thing for a reason, and a medical facility would have plenty worth stealing.

Gabi wasn't helpless—I'd seen her handle herself in tough situations before—but I was definitely glad I was here, even if she didn't want me to be.

"Honestly, I hadn't gotten that far. I just wanted to be here. I hoped my presence alone would be a deterrent." She shrugged, but I saw the tension in her shoulders. "Beyond all that, I wanted to be here so I can help with any emergencies on-island in the wake of the storm. Trees will go down, power lines will snap, and it's gonna be hard to move around. I need to be where the medical equipment is if I'm needed. There's the triage station we set up at the community center, but anything more serious will need the facilities here. Right now, I'm the only doctor around."

That was a hell of a weight to carry, especially for someone who'd just finished her residency and was still finding her footing as an attending physician. But it was so perfectly Gabi —putting everyone else's needs before her own safety.

"I can respect and understand that," I said carefully, "but once the power goes, since we're all the way in here, it's not likely anybody would recognize anyone's here. Cars could be left behind, and the building might appear empty from the outside."

"True. I'm hoping it doesn't come to that." She ate a cracker with cheese and salami. "Thank you for the food and the extra supplies you brought."

In other words, time for a subject change. Message received loud and clear. I could roll with that, even if every instinct I possessed was screaming at me to push harder, to make her talk to me properly.

"Anytime."

For a few more minutes, we ate in silence that felt less hostile and more... careful. Like we were both walking on eggshells, afraid to say the wrong thing and shatter whatever fragile peace we'd managed to build. The storm continued its assault outside, and I found myself cataloging every sound—the way the wind howled around the corners of the building, the rhythmic drumming of rain against the walls, the occasional crash of something being hurled against the structure.

Then, as if someone flipped a switch, the power went out.

The sudden darkness was absolute and disorienting. The constant hum of the air conditioning and fluorescent lights that I hadn't even been aware of suddenly cut off, leaving only the storm's voice.

"Knew it was comin'." Switching on the flashlight on my phone, I fumbled my way to the candles I'd spotted earlier on a supply shelf.

Gabi turned on a battery-powered camp lantern, casting dancing shadows on the walls. By the time I got the half dozen candles lit and set around the room in strategic positions, the space was starting to remind me of another hurricane party, when we'd been trapped alone together in that windowless stairwell.

That had been how we'd met, just a few short weeks into her second year of residency. I'd been visiting a buddy who lived in her building when the evacuation order came too late for anyone to actually leave safely. We'd ended up in that stair-well together—her with a bag of snacks and a bottle of wine, me with a deck of cards and a thermos of coffee. We'd sat together in the humid dark after the power died and talked for hours about everything and nothing. Then we'd found far better things to do with our mouths in the dark.

Shaking off the memory of the best damned make-out session of my life—and everything that had followed over the next two years—I settled back in my chair, the plastic creaking under my weight. "So what's it like being home, Dr. Carrera?"

Her narrow-eyed glare could've cut through steel, and I realized immediately that I'd said something wrong. The formal title, maybe? Or just the fact that I was trying to make small talk when we had so much unfinished business between us?

I scrambled to recover, my words tumbling over each other. "You look good. You look happy. Or you did before I showed up." Might as well acknowledge that I knew I was up shit creek with her without a paddle.

When she only continued to stare at me with those dark eyes that had once looked at me with such warmth, I gave up on finding the right approach. Sometimes the only way forward was straight through, even if it hurt like hell.

"For whatever it's worth, Gabs," I said, my voice rough with emotion I couldn't quite hide, "I'm so fucking sorry."

THIRTEEN

GABI

I stared at him. This man I'd met in a hurricane. The very night I'd been trying desperately not to remember as he'd sucked up all the air in the clinic with his very unwelcome presence. This man I'd let myself fall for, let myself build a future with in my mind, though we'd never overtly defined things between us. We'd started out in a situationship and evolved into more. And it had been as natural as breathing. Maybe that should have been my first warning sign—nothing in my life had ever come easily before. Not my career, not my relationships, not even finding my place back home in Hatterwick after being away for so long.

I'd thought we were on the same page. Then he'd proved I couldn't have been more wrong, shattering my poor, trusting heart.

And now, here he was, dropping an apology that was so beyond overdue, I had no idea what to do with it.

"You're sorry? You're sorry." The words tumbled out of me, edged with a bitter laugh that scraped my throat raw. "Do you even know what you're apologizing for?" Because an apology wasn't an apology without understanding. Without acknowledgment of the specific wounds inflicted.

"For hurting you. I made the wrong fucking choice for damned sure."

The admission hung between us like a bridge I wasn't sure I was ready to cross. It meant something for him to acknowledge his mistake so plainly, without excuses or deflection. To mean it with such obvious conviction. Regret was written all over the face I knew so well, etched into every familiar line and angle. Those dark eyes that crinkled at the corners when he smiled at me, warm and inviting as Louisiana molasses. The strong jawline I'd traced with my fingertips countless times during lazy Sunday mornings in his bed, memorizing the slight roughness of stubble beneath my touch. The face I'd once thought I could read like a book.

But familiarity bred assumptions, and assumptions had led us here. To this broken place where love wasn't enough to bridge the gap his choices had carved between us.

His words weren't enough. Not when I was still raw from how thoroughly he'd blindsided me. Not when the wound was still tender to the touch, barely healed over with scar tissue that pulled tight whenever I thought about what we'd lost.

"You were offered a promotion, and you took it without even discussing it with me." The words came out steady, each one carefully measured. "You made the decision without taking me into account at all, either assuming I'd change the plans I'd been talking to you about for months, or implying that my plans —that I—didn't matter. Do you have any idea what that felt like, Daniel? To go from feeling like the center of your world to realizing I was just an afterthought?"

The ache that had faded these past several weeks to a manageable throb flared bright and sharp again. Like pressing on an unhealed bruise. I fought back tears, the same ones I'd shed in private for weeks after he'd left. All that wasted time and effort and dreams we'd built together, reduced to nothing by his unilateral decision.

He set his plate aside so fast half the food slid onto the floor with a wet splatter, forgotten in his urgency to explain. "Gabi, no. That's not what I meant. Not at all what I intended." His hand started to reach for me—the same instinctive gesture he always made when I was upset, when he wanted to comfort and connect. But he caught himself midway, awareness flickering across his features as he remembered we weren't there anymore. Instead, he tunneled both hands through his thick, dark hair, a nervous habit that used to make me want to smooth those unruly strands back into place.

"I know my intention doesn't mean fuck-all now." His Louisiana accent thickened with emotion the way it always did when he was worked up. "The reality is I hurt you, and I never wanted to do that. Not ever. I was pressured to make a decision real fast—they needed an answer within hours, not days—and I went with impulse. Pure, stupid impulse. I knew it was the wrong impulse pretty much the moment I had time to breathe and think clearly. But by then, I was already on the damned plane and the damage to us was done."

I watched him struggle with the memory, saw the way his shoulders tensed with the weight of regret. Part of me wanted to reach out, to offer the comfort that had always come so naturally between us. But I held myself still, waiting for more. Needing more.

As if exhausted by the confession, he braced his forearms on his knees and leaned toward me. "I was wrong in how I handled it. I was wrong in taking the promotion at all. So much so that I knew within a week of getting there I'd made the biggest mistake of my life. I missed you like crazy, Gabi. Every damn day. And I hated Seattle—the rain, the cold, the way everything felt gray and lifeless. This Southern boy does not need to live so far above the Mason-Dixon line, that's for sure." A ghost of his old smile flickered across his face before fading. "And it's just—it took some doing to orchestrate a transfer to Nag's Head so I could get over here to try to apologize and fix what I broke."

My plate wobbled in suddenly nerveless fingers, nearly following his to the deck. "You're stationed at Nag's Head?" The question came out sharper than I'd intended, surprise cutting through my carefully maintained composure. I'd wondered when I saw him yesterday at the clinic, but I hadn't let myself dwell on the possibility of what it might mean. Hadn't dared to hope.

"Yeah. Kinda took a demotion to do it. But yeah."

The simple words hit me like a physical blow. My heart started to pound, a rapid staccato that echoed in my ears and made it hard to think clearly. This was a big freaking deal—bigger than I'd ever expected. He'd made major changes that went against everything I thought I knew about him. The Daniel I knew was ambitious, driven, always climbing the Coast Guard ladder with single-minded determination. He'd taken a hit on the career that meant so much to him, sacrificed rank and opportunity for... what? For me?

And I had no clue what any of it meant. I mean, he'd already declared he was here for me. He'd changed his life to put me first, to repair what he'd so carelessly broken, even though he couldn't have known what my current position was or whether I'd forgive him at all. For all he knew, I could have moved on completely, could be dating someone else, could slam the door in his face and tell him it was too late.

This was huge. Life-altering. The kind of grand gesture romance novels were built on.

And I had absolutely no idea how I felt about it.

"Why didn't you tell me sooner?" The question slipped out before I thought better of it, tinged with hurt and confusion. "You've been here since yesterday, Daniel. You could have—"

His shoulders lifted in a shrug that managed to be both sheepish and determined. "Well, I wanted to prove I was serious before I came to grovel and apologize. Show you I'd already made changes, not just promise to make them. I'm aware I'm falling down on the groveling portion of the program right about now, but I can work on that if you'll let me." His dark eyes met mine, steady and sure despite the vulnerability I saw lurking beneath. "The essential point here is that I love you, Gabi. I'm in love with you, and I miss the hell out of you. Of us. Of what we had before I screwed it all up."

My breath caught, trapped somewhere between my lungs and my throat. Love. He loved me. The word I'd bitten back a hundred times during our months together, afraid of scaring him off with the intensity of my feelings, afraid of being too much too soon. The word that had threatened to spill out when he'd hold me close after a particularly long shift at the hospital, or when we'd dance in his kitchen to old jazz records while dinner simmered on the stove, or when we lay curled together in bed, talking long into the night about everything and nothing.

I'd known I loved him for months before he'd left. Had ached with it, carried it like a burning coal in my chest that both warmed and scorched me. The emotion had been so overwhelming sometimes that I'd had to bite my tongue to keep from blurting it out during quiet moments. But we'd never said the words. Never crossed that line that would've made everything real and defined instead of existing in that gray area between casual and committed.

Now here he sat on the floor of my clinic, speaking the words that would've changed everything back then. The words that might've made me fight harder when he'd announced his transfer to Seattle. Might've made him reconsider taking it in the first place. Might've given us a foundation strong enough to weather the storm of his ambition and my dreams.

My fingers trembled against the paper plate in my lap, the simple touch suddenly too much to process. The remains of our impromptu hurricane picnic blurred as tears threatened, the colorful array of fruits and sandwiches becoming an impressionist painting through the lens of my unshed emotion. Because I still loved him. God help me, I'd never stopped. I'd buried it deep, tried to forget, tried to move on with my life and my career and my plans for the future. But seeing him again ripped open all those wounds I'd done my best to stitch closed with time and distance and sheer force of will.

But love wasn't always enough. I'd learned that lesson the hard way through watching too many relationships crumble despite the best intentions. Sometimes, timing was everything. And our timing had been spectacularly wrong before—two people pulled in different directions by duty and dreams and the assumption that love alone could bridge any gap.

The question was whether it was right now.

He shifted beside me, drawing in a breath that told me he wasn't finished. That there was more he needed to say, more cards to lay on the table.

"I want another chance, Gabi. I know I don't deserve one after what I put you through. I know it's gonna take a long time to earn back your trust, to prove that I've changed and won't do the same thing again. That I won't take you for granted or make decisions about our future without you ever again." His voice dropped, becoming rougher with emotion. "But despite all that —despite knowing the odds are stacked against me—I'm here. Ready to do whatever it takes to earn my way back into your good graces, however long it takes."

I'd spent so much of the past few months trying to put Daniel LaRue out of my mind. To focus on my own plans for the future, on building my practice at the clinic and reconnecting with my family and the island community that had always held my heart. But a piece of me had still been in New Orleans, mourning the personal future I'd been forced to give up when he'd chosen his career over us.

Suddenly, that future was no longer out of reach. He was here, solid and real and claiming to love me. A man willing and ready to do the hard work of rebuilding what we'd lost, with no guarantee of success. That was a heady offer, the kind that made my romantic heart want to leap without looking. But leaping without looking was how I got into this mess in the first place, and I was nothing if not a woman who learned from her mistakes.

Was there room for him in my life here? In the carefully constructed plans I'd made for my future on Hatterwick?

For all that I'd been very transparent with him about my intention to return home and join the clinic, we'd never discussed a future where he came with me. In a sense, I'd assumed as much as he had about our relationship. But my assumption was that we were on the same page, that he'd want to follow me here when the time came. That we'd make the decision together, as partners should. I wanted to believe I'd have discussed it with him before making firm plans, would have included him in the conversation about our shared future.

That was the difference between us, wasn't it? I believed in talking things through, in careful planning and mutual decisions. Maybe that's why his unilateral choice to take the Seattle position had hurt so much, even though I'd already been planning my return to Hatterwick. The irony wasn't lost on me—we'd both made assumptions, but mine had been about inclusion while his had been about independence.

But even with his transfer to Nag's Head, the logistics were still complicated. Two hours north by boat on a good day, longer when the weather was rough. While that was a damned sight closer than Seattle, it still wasn't exactly commuting distance. Unless he'd been hiding some secret billionaire status and had a helicopter at his disposal, his job still wasn't compatible with living here full time. He couldn't live on Hatterwick any more than I could or would move to the mainland permanently.

Which left us where, exactly? Even accounting for good weather and the fastest ferry service available, the math didn't work in our favor. A four-hour round trip commute would be brutal for anyone, let alone someone in the military who needed to be alert and ready for emergencies at a moment's notice. Daniel's dedication to his Coast Guard duties had always been one of the things I admired about him, but even he didn't have the power to bend the laws of geography and time to make this work.

I realized I'd let the silence stretch too long when he rubbed the back of his neck, another familiar gesture that tugged at my heart.

"I'm realizing now I made another grave miscalculation." His voice carried a rueful note that made me look up at him. "Because you've had every opportunity and right to move on with somebody else. And I've gone and changed my world again without consulting you first." One corner of his mouth quirked in a wry smile that I wanted to taste, wanted to kiss away along with all the hurt between us. "It felt like an appropriately grand gesture at the time. Sorry 'bout that."

It was a grand gesture. The kind that made my chest tight with emotion and possibility. I'd learned long ago that talk was cheap—anyone could make promises when their back was against the wall. But a person's actions told you where they really stood, what they were willing to sacrifice for love. He claimed to love me, and he'd moved heaven and earth to get here to tell me, to prove it with more than just words.

That meant something. It meant everything.

Come on, girl. You miss him, and you love him, too. Are you really going to let a little thing like logistics get in the way of this?

FOURTEEN

DANIEL

Well, I'd gone and fucked up again.

At least I'd made an apology and done something to make things right between us, even if what was right wasn't what I'd been hoping for. What had I expected? That I'd show up with supplies and an apology, and she'd fall into my arms like some romantic movie? That walking away from the Seattle promotion would somehow erase the fact that I'd taken it in the first place without even talking to her about it?

She didn't owe me a second chance just because I finally got my head out of my ass. Hell, she didn't owe me anything at all. I'd made my choice three months ago, picking ambition over us. The fact that I'd realized it was the wrong choice—the worst fucking choice of my life—didn't change what I'd done to us.

My career would recover eventually. The Coast Guard wasn't known for holding grudges against good sailors, and my record spoke for itself. I could do good work here on Hatterwick, serve the community, make a difference. But God almighty, being this close to her and knowing she'd never be mine again? That she'd moved on while I was chasing ghosts in

Seattle? That fucking stung worse than any Louisiana hurricane I'd weathered.

"I'll just—"

My words cut off as Gabi launched herself at me with the force of a rogue wave. Her body collided with mine, the impact sending me toppling backward onto the narrow mattress where I sat. My arms automatically came around her to stop us both from crashing into the wall behind us, muscle memory taking over. Her hands fisted in the fabric of my shirt, desperate and fierce, and then her mouth found mine with a hunger that stole the breath from my lungs.

Thank God. Thank God.

My heart hammered against my ribs like it was trying to break free as the kiss deepened, desperate and hungry, carrying the weight of all our months apart. Outside the clinic, wind howled through the streets of Hatterwick with a fury that matched the storm raging inside my chest, but I barely registered it. My world narrowed to nothing but the press of her body against mine, the taste of her lips—familiar yet somehow brand new, like coming home after being lost at sea.

Her teeth caught my lower lip, tugging with just enough bite to make me groan deep in my throat, and I pulled her closer, needing to eliminate every inch of space between us. One of my hands slid up the length of her back, feeling the tension coiled in her muscles like a spring wound too tight. She arched into my touch like a live wire, electric and dangerous and everything I'd been craving during those long, empty nights in Seattle.

"I hate that I missed you," she breathed against my mouth, the admission torn from somewhere deep inside her.

"I hate that I left." My voice came out rough, raw with emotion I'd been choking down for months. "I hate that I was such a fucking coward."

Thunder cracked overhead like a gunshot, rattling the windows of the clinic and making the emergency lights flicker. Gabi's hands moved to my chest, pushing me flat against the thin mattress with surprising strength. Her dark hair fell around us like a curtain, shutting out the rest of the world as she braced herself above me, her eyes wild and wanting.

"This doesn't fix anything," she warned, but her eyes told a different story entirely—dark and desperate, reflecting the storm that raged both inside the clinic and out on the streets.

I traced my thumb across the sharp line of her cheekbone, memorizing the softness of her skin. "I know."

She kissed me again, harder this time, like she was trying to punish us both for wanting this, for needing each other despite everything that had gone wrong between us. My hands found her hips, steadying her as another thunderclap shook the building to its foundations. The emergency lights flickered again, casting strange, dancing shadows across her face when she pulled back to look at me with those fierce, beautiful eyes.

"Three months, Daniel." Her voice cracked on my name like ice breaking.

"I'm here now." I brushed my lips against the curve of her jaw, felt her shiver despite the warmth between us. "I'm not going anywhere ever again."

She made a sound somewhere between a laugh and a sob, broken and beautiful, and then her mouth was on mine again, stealing my breath, my thoughts, everything except the burning need to be closer, to erase the distance and time that had kept us apart.

Gabi's fingers clawed at my uniform shirt with urgent desperation, pulling it up and over my head in one swift motion. With the same frantic energy, I reached for her, my hands finding the hem of her scrub top. The fabric whispered against her skin as I peeled it off, revealing the smooth curve of her shoulders, the delicate dip of her collarbone, the constellation of freckles I'd memorized long ago. She shivered, but not from cold—from anticipation, from need, from the same fire that was consuming me from the inside out.

Outside, the storm raged with increasing fury, but in here, it was just us, stripped down to the barest, most honest versions of ourselves.

Her hands were at my belt, fingers working quickly with the practiced efficiency of someone who'd done this before, who knew exactly how to undo me. I toed off my boots, the sound unnaturally loud in the small room, and she dragged my pants and boxer briefs down my legs with impatient tugs, until I lay there in nothing but skin and scars and the memories of everything we used to be together.

Gabi leaned back on her heels, her eyes roving over me with a hunger that made my blood run hot, taking in every inch like she was trying to catalog the changes three months had wrought. She reached behind her with graceful movements, unclasped her bra, and let it fall to the floor beside the cot. She rose just long enough to shuck her own jeans and underwear, movements quick and efficient despite the tremor in her hands.

Then she was bare before me, beautiful and fierce and wild, a storm of barely contained passion that I wanted to drown in, wanted to lose myself in completely.

I held out a hand for her, an invitation and a plea rolled into one. Those long, slim, capable fingers closed around mine, warm and sure. She came back down to join me on the narrow mattress, and I pulled her against me with gentle urgency.

Her breath hitched as our bodies pressed together, skin on skin, no barriers, no lies, no more miles between us. Her mouth found mine again, desperate and wild and tasting like home. Her hands were everywhere, tracing the lines of muscles I'd built during long hours of Coast Guard training, the ridges of scars I'd collected over years of service. I explored her body like it was uncharted territory, relearning the curves and valleys, the places that made her gasp, the sensitive spots that made her moan my name like a prayer.

She rolled us over with surprising strength, straddling me, her dark hair falling around us like a protective curtain. Her eyes locked onto mine, fierce and full of fire and something deeper that made my chest tight. "I haven't forgiven you yet," she said, the words both a warning and a promise.

My hands curled around her trembling thighs where they braced above me. "I know," I whispered back. "I don't deserve it yet."

The world narrowed to nothing but Gabi as she slowly, deliberately sank down, taking me inside her body with a control that spoke of both desire and defiance. Her inner walls gripped me so tight and slick and perfectly familiar that it felt like coming home after years lost at sea. Home. Her eyes fluttered closed, a soft gasp escaping her lips as she began to move with a rhythm that was both remembered and brand new.

I gripped her hips as she rode me, glorying in the dance of our bodies finding each other again, muscle memory overriding months of separation. Every movement sent waves of pleasure through me, building and cresting like the storm outside.

She leaned forward, her hair brushing against my chest like silk, her breath hot and ragged on my skin. "Daniel," she whispered, and my name on her lips was a plea and a promise and a benediction all at once. I lifted my hips to meet hers, driving deeper, chasing that edge where pleasure and pain blurred into something transcendent.

Her nails dug into my shoulders, leaving marks I knew I'd treasure later, her pace quickening as desperation took hold. I could hear her breath go short and sharp, her need as desperate and urgent as mine as moved against me, seeking something only I could give her.

Outside, the storm raged with biblical fury, thunder echoing our frantic rhythm, wind howling like a wild thing trying to break down the walls. But in here, it was just us, lost in each other, in the storm we'd created between these four walls.

I groaned her name, my voice ragged and broken. Her eyes met mine, dark and fierce and vulnerable, and I saw it written across her beautiful face—the same raw need that was tearing me apart from the inside. She was close, so close. It was in the tension of her muscles, in the hitch of her breath, in the way her rhythm began to stumble as she rocked and rocked, seeking her release.

I reached between us, finding the sensitive bundle of nerves at her center, circling her clit with my thumb and applying just the right pressure—the touch I remembered she loved, the one that always drove her wild. Her body jerked as if she'd been struck by lightning, a cry tearing from her throat as she came apart in my arms, her inner walls clamping around me like a velvet vise, pulling me over the edge with her into blissful oblivion.

My release slammed into me like a tsunami, waves of pleasure crashing over me in relentless succession, leaving me gasping and spent and completely undone. Gabi collapsed onto my chest, her body trembling with aftershocks, her breath coming in ragged gasps that matched my own. I wrapped my arms around her, holding her close as her heart thundered against mine in perfect synchronization.

We lay there in the aftermath, our bodies slick with sweat, our breaths slowly returning to something resembling normal. The storm outside seemed to have quieted, or maybe it was just that our own personal hurricane was louder, more intense, drowning out everything else. I pressed a kiss to her forehead, tasting the salt of her sweat, feeling the incredible softness of her skin against my lips.

She lifted her head after long minutes, her eyes meeting mine, and I saw the same complex mix of emotions rioting in my chest reflected back at me. Relief and satisfaction, yes, but also uncertainty, the knowledge that this desperate coupling didn't fix everything between us, that there was still so much left unsaid, so much damage left to repair.

But for now, holding her in my arms as the storm raged outside, it was enough. It had to be enough.

FIFTEEN

GABI

I traced lazy circles on Daniel's chest, watching the candlelight flicker across his skin. The storm raged outside with a ferocity that made the reinforced windows of the clinic tremble, but in here everything was still, suspended in time like we existed in our own private universe. My body hummed with satisfaction, muscles loose and relaxed in a way they hadn't been in months.

"You okay?" Daniel's voice rumbled under my fingertips, the deep vibration traveling through his chest and into my palm.

I nodded against his shoulder, breathing in the familiar scent of his skin mixed with the faint antiseptic smell that seemed to permeate every corner of the clinic. The physical connection had always been easy between us—passionate, electric, like touching a live wire. That wasn't what broke us apart. Sex had never been our problem; it was everything else that came crashing down around us.

"This doesn't fix everything," I whispered against the warm curve of his shoulder, the words muffled but necessary.

"I know." His hand stroked down my back, fingers trailing

along my spine in a way that sent shivers racing through me despite the humid air trapped inside the clinic.

Thoughts churning like the storm outside, I pressed closer to Daniel's warmth, breathing in the scent of salt air and that hint of cedar that always clung to him, as if the Louisiana bayous had permanently marked him as their own. I wanted to melt into him, to pretend the past months of hurt and anger and sleepless nights had never happened, that we could somehow rewind to those early days when everything seemed possible.

But they had happened. The sex was incredible—always had been, from that very first night when we'd practically set his apartment on fire with the intensity of our connection. Yet, in the quiet aftermath, with only the sound of our breathing and the distant roar of Hurricane Hannah, doubt crept back in like floodwater seeping through the cracks. Could I trust him not to bulldoze over my dreams again? Did coming here, to this island that meant everything to me, mean he finally understood why this place, this life, mattered so much to me?

"I missed you." His murmur was warm against my temple.

"I missed you, too." The words slipped out before I could stop them, honest and raw. True, but dangerous in their simplicity. Missing someone wasn't enough of a foundation to rebuild on, not when the cracks in our relationship ran so deep. Neither was stupendous sex, no matter how my body still sang from his touch. We'd both need more than that to turn this into something real, something lasting.

The wind howled outside with renewed fury, rattling the clinic's reinforced windows and making the emergency lights flicker ominously. I shivered, despite the still, humid air trapped inside the clinic's sealed corridors. Daniel grabbed one of the thin cotton blankets I'd gathered from patient rooms and draped it over us, the institutional fabric rough against my sensitized skin. His arms felt like home as they encircled me, and that terrified me almost as much as the storm bearing down on us with all its destructive power.

A loud bang jolted me from my spiraling thoughts, the sound cutting through the storm's constant roar like a gunshot. Daniel's body went rigid beside me, every muscle suddenly taut with alertness.

My heart hammered against my ribs as adrenaline flooded my system. "What was that?"

Daniel relaxed a fraction, though tension still coiled in his shoulders. "Probably just debris from the storm."

That was the most logical explanation. Hurricane winds of this magnitude would be tossing around anything that wasn't properly secured outside—tree branches, patio furniture, signs torn from their mountings. The island was probably littered with projectiles by now.

But what if it wasn't debris? What if it was something more sinister?

"What if someone's trying to break in again?" The words tumbled out, giving voice to the fear that had been gnawing at me since yesterday. The memory of the jimmied lock flashed through my mind with crystal clarity.

Daniel was already moving, yanking on his cargo pants. I scrambled for my clothes, fingers fumbling with buttons and zippers as adrenaline coursed through my system like liquid lightning. I managed to yank on my jeans and shirt just as another bang echoed through the clinic, closer this time and definitely more deliberate than random debris.

My hand found Daniel's arm, gripping tight enough to leave marks. The muscle beneath my fingers was coiled like a spring, ready for action.

"Stay here," he hissed, his voice taking on an authoritative edge.

"Like hell." The words came out sharper than I intended,

but I wasn't about to cower in the break room while someone potentially ransacked my workplace.

Eyes narrowed in frustration, he indicated with a sharp gesture that I should stay close behind him as we crept out of the break room and into the main hallway. Emergency lights cast eerie shadows along the corridor, transforming the space I knew like the back of my hand into something alien and threatening. Our bare feet made no sound on the cold tile floor as we eased down the hall, every sense straining to catch the slightest hint of an intruder's presence.

Another crash sounded, definitely closer this time and accompanied by what might have been a muffled curse. Daniel pressed me back against the wall, his body forming a protective barrier between me and whatever lay ahead. We waited for endless seconds that dragged like hours, the only sounds our carefully controlled breathing and the storm's relentless assault on the building's exterior.

At last, he backed off slightly, and we eased down the hall with painstaking care, peering around the corner toward the back entrance that led to the clinic's service area.

The metal door swung wildly on its hinges, slamming against the wall with each powerful gust of wind that tore through the opening. Rain sprayed inside in sheets, forming expanding puddles on the floor.

That door had been locked—I'd checked it myself when we'd done our final security sweep before settling in for the night. It was conceivable that something might have struck it with enough force to knock it open, but peering into the darkness just outside the open door, I didn't see evidence of a tree branch or other large debris that would account for the damage.

Daniel gestured toward something on the floor, his movements careful and controlled. I squinted, angling my head until my mind made sense of the dark splotches scattered across the tile in front of me.

Wet footprints. Someone else was here, someone who had no business being in the clinic during a hurricane.

Daniel's hand wrapped around mine, tugging me back. His lips brushed my ear, his breath warm against my skin as he whispered, "Where are the drugs kept?"

"Central hall, a room across from Exam Three. Steel door, no windows, keypad entry." My voice came out barely above a breath, the words almost lost in the storm's fury.

He nodded grimly. "Anyone else have the code?"

"Just Dr. Sibley and our head nurse. But the keypad won't work with the power outage—it's not on the backup system."

Meaning the intruder likely wouldn't be able to get to what he came for, assuming the pharmaceutical supplies were indeed his target. The clinic's drug lockup was built like a fortress specifically to prevent break-ins, with steel-reinforced walls and electronic locks that required both a valid code and active power to the security system.

We crept down the hallway, my heart pounding so hard I worried the intruder might hear it echoing off the walls. Daniel moved like a predator, each step calculated and silent, his Coast Guard training obvious in every controlled movement. I tried to match his careful progression, but my bare feet stuck slightly to the cold tile floor with each step.

A clatter from the supply closet down the hall froze us both in place. Daniel immediately pushed me behind him, pressing us both against the wall. He held up three fingers, then two, then one, counting down before we moved.

We burst around the corner in perfect synchronization. Empty. But the closet door stood ajar, and supplies were scattered across the floor in disarray—bandages, syringes, tongue depressors all strewn about as if someone had been searching for something specific and growing increasingly frustrated when they didn't find it.

"They're working their way toward the exam rooms," Daniel whispered, his voice barely audible above the storm.

My stomach clenched with dread. If they found the drug lockup and somehow managed to breach it, we'd lose thousands of dollars worth of controlled substances—medications that the island's residents desperately needed, especially with the hurricane potentially isolating us for days.

A shadow moved at the end of the hall, barely visible in the emergency lighting's glow. Daniel's arm shot out, shoving me into a shallow alcove where we normally took patient vitals. His body pressed against mine, completely shielding me as footsteps approached with deliberate, measured cadence.

The power flickered ominously, plunging us into complete darkness for two terrifying heartbeats before the emergency lights sputtered back on with a faint electrical hum.

The footsteps stopped abruptly.

I held my breath until my lungs burned. Daniel's muscles coiled tight against me like a compressed spring. Ready to move. Ready to protect. Ready to do whatever it took to keep us both safe.

The metallic thud of something heavy striking the drug lockup door echoed down the hallway like a gunshot. My fingers dug into Daniel's arm as we listened to repeated impacts, each one more frustrated and violent than the last, the sound of someone losing patience.

"Damn it!" A male voice growled, rough and edged with desperation. More strikes against the reinforced door followed, then an ominous silence that was somehow more threatening than the noise.

Daniel's breath was warm against my neck as we stayed frozen in the alcove, barely daring to breathe.

Another crash, followed by a string of creative cursing that would have made a sailor blush. "Why's the fucking backup generator not on?"

My decision to save the generator for a genuine emergency might have just saved our drug supply. But we were still trapped in here with a criminal who was growing increasingly desperate and unpredictable. Daniel's body remained tense against mine, ready to move at any moment. But moving meant revealing our position, and as long as the intruder remained focused on that impenetrable door, we were safer staying hidden in our shallow alcove.

Footsteps paced back and forth in front of the drug room, wet shoes squeaking against the tile floor in an agitated rhythm. "There's gotta be another way in."

Daniel's hand found mine, squeezing once with gentle pressure. A silent question: *ready to move if we need to?*

I squeezed back without hesitation. *Yes.*

The sound of doors being thrown open with increasing violence grew closer as our unwelcome visitor began methodically searching each room. He was working his way systematically toward us, checking every possible hiding spot and alternative entrance. The alcove wouldn't hide us for much longer. We were running out of time and options.

A beam of bright light swept past our hiding spot like a searchlight. Daniel's muscles tensed against me, his body coiled like a predator preparing to strike. The intruder's footsteps squeaked against the floor, drawing nearer to our alcove with each step.

A shadow fell across us as the figure approached. The moment he stepped into view, flashlight beam sweeping toward our hiding spot, Daniel exploded into action. He drove his shoulder into the man's midsection with devastating force, tackling him backward and sending them both crashing into the opposite wall.

The flashlight spun across the floor, casting wild, disorienting shadows as it rolled. The beam swept crazily across walls and ceiling before coming to rest pointed down the hall, providing just enough illumination to see the struggle unfolding.

I pressed myself flat against the wall, heart hammering so hard I felt my pulse in my throat as the two men grappled with brutal intensity. Fists flew in the confined space, bodies slammed against walls with sickening thuds. The intruder was shorter than Daniel but stocky and powerful, matching Daniel's height advantage with raw, desperate strength.

They crashed into a supply cart, sending it clattering across the floor in an explosion of medical supplies. The emergency lights flickered with each impact against the walls, casting everything in surreal, strobing shadows that made it nearly impossible to track their movements clearly.

A grunt of pain echoed through the hallway as the intruder caught Daniel with a vicious elbow to the face. Blood immediately began trickling from his nose.

Daniel stumbled, his grip loosening just enough for the other man to gain advantage. The intruder seized his chance, shoving Daniel hard toward the scattered supplies from the overturned cart. Daniel's feet tangled in the debris, and he went down hard, his head striking the floor with a sound that made me want to scream.

The intruder bolted immediately, shoes squealing on the wet floor as he sprinted for the exit. Daniel scrambled up despite the blood now flowing freely from his nose, shaking his head to clear it.

"Stay here!" he shouted over his shoulder.

Before I uttered another word, before I could beg him not to go, they'd both disappeared through the open door and straight into the belly of the storm, still raging outside with undiminished fury. Lightning flashed brilliantly, illuminating their silhouettes for a split second before darkness swallowed them again, and I was left alone and terrified.

SIXTEEN

DANIEL

The rain stung my bare skin like a thousand angry wasps as I chased the shadow ahead through sheets of wind-driven water that seemed to come from every direction at once. My feet scraped against rough, debris-strewn pavement, each step sending jolts of pain up my legs, but adrenaline dulled everything except the burning need to catch this bastard. That face—I'd stared at his mugshot for hours during briefings back at the station. Mickey Doyle. Street dealer with a rap sheet longer than my arm. According to intel, he usually worked the pier bars all along the Outer Banks, slinging whatever poison would make him a quick buck. Suspicion was that he had connections higher up the chain that we hadn't mapped yet, connections that might lead us to the real players in this operation.

A branch whipped past my head, close enough that bark scraped my cheek. The wind howled like something alive and furious, drowning out everything except the blood roaring in my ears.

My mind raced faster than my feet, questions tumbling over each other in rapid succession. What the hell was he doing at the clinic? Our intelligence suggested the operation moved product through fishing boats and waterfront bars, not medical facilities. And the product they moved was generally cocaine or fentanyl—street drugs with high profit margins. Had they started branching out, looking for prescription drugs? Oxy, morphine, anything they could get their hands on? Or was this simply a crime of opportunity?

A piece of debris—looked like part of a fence post—slammed into my shoulder with enough force to spin me halfway around. I stumbled, nearly going down on one knee, but kept moving. Mickey was fading into the darkness ahead, his form barely visible through the curtain of rain. The storm made it impossible to see more than a few feet in any direction. Thunder cracked overhead like the world splitting open, and a sudden gust all but knocked me sideways into a parked car.

This was insane. No shoes, no shirt, no weapon, chasing a suspect through the outer bands of a Category 3 hurricane. But Mickey could be our break. I hadn't been here for the months of dead ends and careful surveillance already conducted by the task force. They'd brought me in as fresh eyes, someone who might spot what the locals had missed. This could crack things open. Give us new avenues to pursue, new leads to follow. If I just managed to keep him in sight.

Another flash of lightning illuminated Mickey ducking behind a weathered bait shop, its hand-painted sign swinging wildly in the wind. I adjusted course, ignoring the bite of broken shells and God knew what else beneath my feet. The wind was picking up even more, blasting my skin with stinging sand and salt spray. But I couldn't lose him. Not now. Not when we were this close.

I rounded the corner of a bait shop at full sprint, my shoulder scraping against the rough wooden siding. Mickey's rigid arm caught me across the chest, clothes-lining me like something out of a wrestling match. My breath exploded out of me as I staggered back, stars dancing in my vision, but training kicked in. I dropped low, finding my balance again and dodging his next wild swing as I drove my shoulder into his midsection with everything I had.

We crashed into a towering stack of crab pots with a sound like a car wreck. The metal cages clattered around us as we grappled, their wire mesh scraping against my bare skin. Mickey fought like a cornered animal, all elbows and knees and desperate fury. One sharp elbow caught me square in the ribs, and I tasted copper in my mouth where I'd bitten my tongue.

A flash of lightning showed his face inches from mine, twisted in desperation and something that might have been panic. I managed to get an arm around his neck, trying for a chokehold, but the rain made everything slick. He slammed an elbow back into my gut, and I felt my picnic dinner try to make a reappearance.

My grip loosened just enough. Mickey twisted free with the desperation of a man facing prison time and scrambled up, kicking at my hands as I tried to grab his ankles. I lunged for his legs but only caught air and a face full of sandy water. He kicked out toward my face, and I jerked back, only barely avoiding a boot to the teeth. As my quarry bolted toward the marina, I pushed to my feet, spitting blood and seawater. The wind howled between the buildings like a banshee, creating a wind tunnel effect that nearly knocked me over again. But I couldn't lose him. Not when he was this close. Whether he was the break that the task force needed or not, I was taking this bastard down to find out whether Gabi was in any further danger.

I sprinted after his retreating form, my feet finding purchase on the wet pavement through sheer determination. We'd left the main road of the village and made it all the way to the marina, where the real danger began. Deck boards creaked ominously under our feet as we raced past the covered slips, the sound barely audible over the storm. Waves crashed against the pilings with increasing violence, sending spray across the walkway that made every step treacherous. Mickey was fast, I had to give him that, but I was gaining ground with each stride.

He glanced back over his shoulder, and another lightning flash illuminated the fear on his face—real terror now, not just the panic of being caught. Then he vaulted over the railing toward one of the boats, a move born of desperation rather than strategy. I followed without hesitation, my body moving on instinct, hitting the deck of the vessel hard enough to rattle my teeth. Mickey scrambled past the cabin like a man possessed, and I launched myself after him without thinking about what I'd do when I caught him.

My shoulder slammed into Mickey's legs as he tried to climb onto the bow, and I didn't know where the fuck he thought he was going in this storm. The ocean was a churning mass of whitecaps and fury that would swallow us both without a second thought. We crashed onto the deck, sliding across the rain-slicked surface as the boat pitched beneath us like a wild horse. The boat rocked violently as waves battered its hull, each impact sending shudders through the fiberglass. Mickey's elbow caught me on the side of the head, stars exploding behind my eyes, but I managed to keep my grip around his waist.

He thrashed like a hooked fish, trying to break free with every ounce of strength he had left. My fingers found purchase on his soaked jacket, the cheap material already starting to tear under the strain. The fabric only bunched around his arms as he tried to twist out of it like some kind of escape artist. I yanked him back as he attempted to crawl away, using his own momentum to flip him over. His head cracked against the deck with a sound that made me wince.

"Stay down!" I rolled him over, pressing my knee into his back to pin him while I caught my breath.

Mickey bucked and twisted beneath me like a bronco. "Get off me, you fucking psycho!"

Ignoring the assortment of bruises no doubt blooming everywhere from our fight, I grabbed his wrist, wrenching it behind his back hard enough to make him yelp. My free hand searched the deck frantically, finding a coil of rope secured to a cleat. I yanked it free, the rough fibers burning my palms as I wrapped it around his wrists. The wet line bit into my hands as I pulled it tight, making sure the knots would hold even if he dislocated his shoulders trying to get free.

"You're under arrest," I growled, securing the knots despite his continued struggles. "For breaking and entering, attempted theft, assault on a federal officer—" The wail of the wind carried away the rest of my litany of charges, but it didn't matter. I was technically on the water, which meant I had jurisdiction until I transferred him to local law enforcement.

"I want a lawyer," Mickey gasped, his voice muffled by the deck.

"Smart choice." I made what amounted to a leash out of the remaining rope, testing the knots one more time. "Though running into a hurricane wasn't your brightest move. What were you thinking?"

Mickey went limp beneath me, finally accepting defeat as the reality of his situation sank in. The wind screamed around us as I caught my breath, rain hammering against my back like bullets. I needed to get him back to the clinic before the storm got any worse. And I had some questions that couldn't wait for the weather to clear.

The boat pitched hard to starboard, tilting at an angle that made my stomach lurch. I grabbed the railing with one hand, keeping Mickey pinned with the other as water sloshed across the deck. We needed off this death trap before the storm ripped it loose from its moorings and sent us both to the bottom of the sound.

"Up," I ordered, hauling Mickey to his feet with more force than was probably necessary. He swayed, unsteady with his arms bound behind his back and his balance shot from the head impact.

I half-dragged him toward the pier, timing our move between wave surges that threatened to wash us both overboard. The gap between boat and dock looked wider with each passing second as the vessel strained against its mooring lines. Mickey stumbled at the edge, nearly taking us both down into the churning water below.

"Gonna have to jump," I shouted over the wind.

"Are you fucking crazy?" Mickey's voice cracked with terror.

"'Course I am. I'm Cajun. We're all crazy. Now jump!" I half threw him over the railing as another wave lifted the boat, sending it crashing back down with bone-jarring force. Mickey landed hard on the pier, rolling toward the edge like a sack of potatoes. I leaped after him, catching his jacket just as he started to slide off the side. The fabric stretched, threatening to tear as I pulled him back from a fifteen-foot drop into churning water that would have killed him in seconds.

Mickey thrashed against my grip, panic making him stupid. "I can't swim like this!"

"Then stop fighting," I snarled, yanking him upright and keeping a firm hold on his arm. "Walk, or I carry you." I wasn't sure how I'd manage the latter, because now that the adrenaline was starting to fade, I felt all the cuts and slices I'd taken to my bare feet during the pursuit. Each step was like walking on broken glass.

He chose to walk, though 'walking' was generous. The wind

hit us full force on the exposed pier, driving needles of rain sideways with enough force to sting like hail. I had to grab the railing twice to keep us both from being blown over the side. Mickey stumbled again, this time taking us both down to our knees. My kneecap cracked against the weathered boards hard enough to bring tears to my eyes.

"Get up," I growled, hauling him back to his feet with hands that were starting to shake from cold and exhaustion.

We fought our way forward step by agonizing step, the wind trying to push us back with each move we made. My bare feet found every splinter and nail head in the weathered boards. The rain was so heavy I could barely breathe without choking on water, and visibility was down to maybe ten feet on a good moment. Mickey kept slipping on the slick surface. His bound arms made it impossible to catch himself, forcing me to practically carry him, anyway.

A massive gust caught us broadside, strong enough to lift Mickey off his feet for a second. I slammed him against a piling, shielding him with my body as debris whipped past—pieces of shingles, palm fronds, what looked like someone's patio furniture. Something sharp caught my back, opening up a line of fire across my shoulder blade, but I held on until the gust passed.

"Move," I growled in his ear, shoving him forward again. There were still at least three blocks between here and the clinic, and the storm was getting worse by the minute.

Mickey's resistance had shifted from active fighting to dead weight, making the journey even harder. He was dragging his feet, probably hoping I'd give up and let him go. My feet were completely numb now, probably bleeding from a dozen cuts, but I didn't dare check. Every second we stayed out here increased our chances of being killed by flying debris or swept away by the storm surge.

A loose shutter exploded off a nearby building, the metal

frame spinning through the air like a giant throwing star. I yanked Mickey down as wooden shards flew past, one piece embedding itself in a telephone pole inches from where his head had been. He took advantage of my split-second distraction, ramming his shoulder into my sternum with everything he had left. The rope burned through my hands as he bolted, his feet slipping and sliding on the wet pavement.

"Dammit!" I scrambled up, ignoring the stabbing pain in my feet and the fire in my lungs.

Mickey made it maybe three steps before a palm frond the size of a dinner table caught him square in the face, knocking him backwards like he'd been hit by a truck. He sprawled on the pavement, his head bouncing off the asphalt with a sound that made me wince. I pounced, driving my knee into his kidney hard enough to make him cry out. He bucked weakly, but I had leverage this time.

"Try that again," I snarled, tightening the rope until he gasped, "and I'll hogtie you and drag you behind me like a sled."

The clinic was only half a block away now, its emergency lighting barely visible through the storm. I could probably manage to carry him that far if I had to, though my back was screaming and my feet felt like hamburger.

"Last chance," I said, hauling him up by his collar. "Walk, or I drag you by your ankles."

Apparently, that last fall had knocked most of the fight out of him. Mickey stumbled forward like a broken puppet, his resistance finally crushed by the reality of the situation. The last few yards to the clinic were a blur of wind and rain and pure determination until suddenly Gabi was there, wielding what looked like an IV pole like a quarterstaff. She'd thrown on rain gear and boots at some point, looking like some kind of medical warrior.

"Get inside!" she shouted over the howling wind, her voice barely audible.

I half-dragged, half-carried my captive toward the door, Mickey's feet barely touching the ground. My legs were shaking with exhaustion, but we were almost there.

Gabi kept the pole trained on Mickey as we stumbled past, her eyes wide with a mixture of relief and fury, then slammed the door against the howling wind with both hands. The sudden quiet was almost deafening. Water pooled around us on the tile floor as she locked the door, her hands shaking slightly.

She whirled on me, brandishing the pole like she was ready to use it. "Are you fucking *insane?*"

SEVENTEEN

GABI

"Not crazy. Just motivated."

The lantern light cast harsh shadows as Daniel hauled our intruder down the hallway. Blood trickled from a cut above the guy's eye. Given the look of both of them, that might have happened more than once. Or perhaps it was all the debris that would've battered them both from their mad dash through the hurricane. The captive's shoes squeaked against the linoleum, leaving wet tracks from the rain they'd brought in. Even in the emergency lights, I saw the cuts on Daniel's bare feet. They left spots of blood on the floor as he walked.

I followed them into the break room, where Daniel shoved the man into one of the metal chairs. The stranger's dirty blonde hair plastered to his forehead, water dripping down his face. His eyes darted between us, but he kept his mouth shut while Daniel secured the man's already bound hands behind the chair. Then he retrieved yet more rope from his supplies and set to work on his legs.

"Hold the light closer," Daniel ordered, as he worked on securing the guy's ankles.

I lifted the lantern, getting my first good look at our captive's face. Mid-thirties, with a scraggly beard and a small scar near his chin. Not someone I recognized from the island. But I'd been gone a long time and working so much that unless the guy had come through the clinic, I wouldn't necessarily have seen him.

Daniel stepped back, his chest heaving. Blood trickled down his back from a gash and from his nose. A bruise was already blooming on his shoulder. His knuckles were raw and bleeding. The adrenaline must have masked the pain until now because he winced when he tried to flex his hand.

"Sit." The word snapped out like a whip, driven by all the fear and adrenaline that had crashed over me when I'd watched the man I loved, the man I'd only just gotten back in my life, race out into the middle of a fucking hurricane. My voice carried the sharp edge of barely controlled panic, years of medical training warring with the primal terror of almost losing him again.

With a wary eye on the captive, Daniel dropped into a chair across the room, his movements stiff and careful. I spotted the exhaustion beginning to seep into his shoulders now that the immediate danger was past. I set down the lantern with trembling hands and reached first for his injured hand, my fingers assessing the damage even as my mind reeled.

"I'm fine." But he didn't pull away when I examined his split knuckles, the skin torn and raw across his middle and ring fingers. Fresh blood still seeped from the deeper cuts. "Check him first."

The cut above our intruder's eye was no longer actively bleeding, but it would need cleaning to prevent infection. As I moved closer with my medical kit, fishing out antiseptic wipes, he jerked his head away like a cornered animal.

"Hold still," I said, my voice shifting into the calm, professional tone I used with difficult patients at the clinic. "That needs antiseptic, or it'll get infected."

The guy's brows drew together as I cleaned the wound, dabbing away the blood and debris, as if he didn't understand why I was still treating him like a human being despite what he'd just put us through. His eyes kept darting between Daniel and me, calculating, waiting for some kind of retaliation that wasn't coming.

"Do you have any other injuries I can't see? Any other cuts or bruising?" I asked, running through my standard patient assessment even though every instinct screamed at me to get away from this man who'd threatened our safety.

"Sure, I've got plenty of both." He managed a leer that didn't quite reach his eyes, which remained sharp and watchful. "You wanna untie me for a head-to-toe inspection, sweetheart?"

"Not happening, Mickey," Daniel growled from across the room, his voice carrying a dangerous edge I'd seldom heard before.

Mickey? He'd learned the guy's name sometime during their violent struggle outside? The casual way Daniel used it suggested this wasn't their first interaction, or at least that Mickey wasn't a complete unknown to him.

Deciding the onus was on the reluctant patient to disclose anything else that needed immediate medical attention, I turned back to Daniel, my concern shifting to the man whose blood was still trickling down his back.

"What in God's name were you thinking running out there *into a hurricane without a shirt or shoes?*" My voice rose an octave, cracking with the strain of holding back tears, and I lapsed into the rapid-fire Spanish my parents had spoken while I was growing up, shooting a litany of colorful insults about

Daniel's intelligence and decision-making abilities that would have made my mother wash my mouth out with soap.

He sat placidly listening to the torrent until I fell silent, exhausting my vocabulary of creative curses. His calm acceptance of my verbal assault only made me angrier. "I was thinkin' that I wasn't about to let a threat to you get away to hurt you another day."

I yanked the medical kit closer with more force than necessary, supplies rattling inside, and pulled out gauze and antiseptic with shaking fingers. "You're an idiot. A complete and total idiot." My hands betrayed me, trembling as I dabbed at his nose, gently probing to check for breaks in the cartilage or bone. "You could have died out there, Daniel. You could have fucking died."

"Gabi—"

"No, shut up." I tilted his chin with two fingers, examining the purple bruising already blooming across his cheekbone and jaw. "There are pieces of who knows what embedded in your feet because you ran out there without shoes like some kind of action movie hero." The words came out harsher than I intended, but I couldn't seem to modulate my tone through the fear still coursing through my system.

His feet were an absolute mess when I got a good look at them. Cuts crisscrossed the soles, some deep enough to require stitches under normal circumstances. Splinters of wood, fragments of shell, pieces of debris I couldn't even identify were embedded in the torn skin. I grabbed tweezers from my kit and started the painstaking work of extracting each piece, my stomach clenching tighter with every fragment I pulled free. "What if you'd stepped on a nail? Or gotten impaled by flying debris? Or been struck by lightning? Or—"

"Hey." His voice was gentle as he caught my wrist, his thumb brushing over my pulse point. "I'm right here. I'm okay."

I yanked free and grabbed more gauze with more force than necessary, my movements jerky with leftover adrenaline. "Turn around. Let me see your back."

The slice across his back wasn't deep enough to require sutures, but it was long and angry-looking. I swabbed it with antiseptic, ignoring Daniel's sharp intake of breath as the alcohol hit the raw wound. "Your ribs are already bruising. Take a deep breath for me."

He inhaled, wincing a little as his ribcage expanded. I pressed along the bones, checking for obvious breaks or displacement.

"Probably just bruised, not broken. But you're lucky it's not worse." My voice snapped as I used irritation to cover how close I was to falling apart. "Do you have any idea what it was like watching you disappear into that storm? Not knowing if you'd come back? Not knowing if I'd ever see you again?"

"About as bad as realizing I might lose you again when I just found you?" His voice was soft, roughened with emotion that matched my own.

I pressed my forehead against his uninjured shoulder, breathing in the scent of rain and antiseptic and something uniquely him that I'd missed more than I could put into words. "Don't ever do that to me again. Promise me."

"Which part? The hurricane chase or the leaving?"

"Either. Both." I straightened and reached for more gauze. "Now hold still while I finish patching you up, you reckless idiot."

When I was finished with the immediate wound care, Daniel dug dry clothes out of his emergency pack and changed with careful movements. He'd be sore for days, probably weeks, but all of it would heal well enough, so long as he avoided infection and didn't do anything else monumentally stupid.

As I cleaned up and reordered my supplies—a ritual that

always helped calm my nerves—Daniel pulled a chair closer to Mickey. The professional mask was sliding back into place, and I saw the Coast Guard officer emerging from behind the man who'd just held me like his world depended on it.

Daniel's voice shifted into an unfamiliar interrogation tone. "So, what was the plan? Wait for the storm, hit the clinic while everyone's hunkered down and defenseless?"

Mickey stared at a point on the wall behind us, his jaw set in stubborn silence.

"Or maybe you had bigger plans." Daniel leaned forward slightly, his posture casual but somehow threatening. "Maybe you were supposed to meet someone here. The Lowe brothers, perhaps?"

My hands stilled on the supplies I was repacking as I caught the subtle flicker that crossed Mickey's face. That name clearly meant something to him, struck some kind of nerve.

"Fuck you," Mickey spat, but there was less venom in it now and more wariness.

"No? How about Heneghan? Or does Ortiz run this particular operation these days?"

Each name Daniel threw out landed like a stone in my stomach. These weren't random shots in the dark or lucky guesses. Daniel knew these people, or at least was aware of them and their connections. This level of knowledge spoke to something much bigger than a simple break-in attempt.

"You Coast Guard types think you know everything." Mickey's lip curled, but his eyes had gone sharp and calculating.

"I know enough." Daniel's voice stayed steady, controlled, utterly professional in a way that made my skin crawl. "The patterns are obvious. Gulf Coast to Eastern Seaboard. Using major weather events as cover for movement. Switching up routes and timing to avoid detection patterns."

The pieces were clicking together in my head with horrible

clarity. The convenient transfer to Nag's Head. The pointed questions about previous break-in attempts at the clinic. His presence on Hatterwick during what should have been a routine hurricane response.

"This isn't just about hurricane response, is it?" The words tumbled out, my voice a whisper.

Daniel's shoulders tensed, but he didn't turn around to face me. "Not now, Gabi."

"You're here on an investigation." The medical kit slipped from my fingers, clattering to the floor and spilling supplies across the linoleum. "That's why you're here. Not for hurricane relief. Not for me. For work."

His silence stretched between us like a chasm, and it was answer enough. How could I have been so fucking stupid? He'd made a name for himself in his Gulf Coast posting specifically for drug interdiction work. What were the actual odds that some appropriate posting at Nag's Head just *happened* to show up right when he claimed he wanted to get out of Seattle and closer to me?

"Gabi, whatever's going through your head right now, it's not the whole truth."

"And what is the truth? Hm?" My voice went sharper, more brittle. "What's the part you conveniently left out?"

"It's complicated."

God, after everything having been so beautifully simple between us during those perfect days in New Orleans, would we ever have anything in our lives come easily again? Was I destined to always be the complication he had to work around?

"Uncomplicate it," I demanded, crossing my arms over my chest. "Right now."

Daniel glanced meaningfully at Mickey, and I saw the internal struggle playing out across his features. He was reluctant to leave our captive alone and unguarded, but just as reluctant to have this conversation in front of someone who was connected to whatever case had brought him here.

"Hall." I didn't wait to see if he'd follow my lead. There was no other exit from the break room. Even if Mickey somehow managed to get loose from his restraints, he couldn't get past us if we positioned ourselves just outside the door.

I turned my back and walked out into the hallway, my bare feet silent on the cold floor. Behind me, Daniel explained to Mickey in no uncertain terms what would happen if he so much as thought about trying to escape.

A few moments later, Daniel joined me in the corridor, pulling the door not quite closed behind him but leaving it open enough that we could hear any movement from inside. He positioned himself strategically between me and the door, still on guard even as he prepared to have what was no doubt going to be a hard conversation.

"My position here is part of a joint task force between the Coast Guard and local law enforcement," he began, his voice measured. "We're attempting to identify and dismantle a drug trafficking organization that's been operating in this area. My experience and skills in that particular arena are what got me the transfer to Nag's Head. So yes, I am here on Hatterwick at this specific time in part because of an ongoing investigation, in addition to legitimate hurricane prep and relief operations."

I dragged a hand through my damp hair, pushing the tangled strands away from my face. Work. It always came down to fucking work with him. His career aspirations, his professional goals, his duty and obligations to everyone except me.

"So this is just a convenient bonus, then?" The words tasted bitter and sharp on my tongue. "Getting to see me while you're here doing your real job? Killing two birds with one stone?"

"That's not fair." Daniel reached for me, but I shifted away before he made contact. "Yes, the task force assignment got me the transfer. But I requested this posting because of you, Gabi. I've been trying to find a way back to you since the day I got on that plane to Seattle."

"And you didn't think to mention this little detail earlier? When you first showed up here? When we—" I cut myself off, not wanting to think about what had happened between us barely an hour ago. How real it had felt in the moment. How much I'd let myself believe that this time might be different.

"You were barely speaking to me when I got here," he said, running a hand through his own disheveled hair. "I had to start somewhere, and beginning with the personal stuff and a genuine apology seemed like the most important thing. The most honest thing." His jaw tightened with frustration. "Look, I know I keep fuckin' things up with you, and I know my timing is shit. But I meant everything I said to you. I am here on the Outer Banks for you. The case just happens to be the vehicle that made it possible. I can't apologize for that, and I can't promise that sometimes the job won't have to come first. But Gabi, I'm doing everything I know how to try to fix this mess between us."

A tremendous crash of thunder rattled the windows hard enough to make the glass flex in the frames, causing us both to jump. The storm continued to rage outside with undiminished fury, but it felt like nothing compared to the tempest raging in my chest.

I crossed my arms tighter, hugging myself against the chill and the hurt. "So what happens when this case is over? When you've caught your bad guys and earned your commendations? When the next big career opportunity comes along?"

"I'll figure something out." His voice carried a note of desperation. "It's a big case with a lot of moving pieces and connected criminal organizations. We're not gonna topple the whole thing in a matter of weeks or even months. And by the time we do make significant progress, my current contract will be up for renewal. I can choose not to re-up. I can get out entirely."

I stared at him in shock. "You'd... leave the Coast Guard? For me?"

"If it comes down to that choice, yes. Because I love you, Gabriella, and I'm tired of pretending that anything else matters more than that."

The words hit me like a physical blow. I wanted him to prove himself with actions rather than just words, and walking away from the career that meant the world to him would certainly qualify as a significant gesture. Of course, it was all hypothetical at this point, easy to promise when the moment of truth was months or years away. But the fact that he'd even consider it, that he'd voice it out loud, spoke volumes about how much this—how much I—meant to him.

Feeling a little more reassured but still wary, I blew out a long breath. "And those questions you were asking in there? All that stuff about the Lowe brothers and the other names? That was all connected to this task force investigation?"

"Unfortunately, yes. It turns out our uninvited guest in there has come up in several of my briefings." Daniel's expression darkened. "I don't like the fact that he's connected to a much bigger drug trafficking ring and that he targeted the clinic tonight. That's not a coincidence I'm comfortable with."

A chill that had nothing to do with the storm ran down my spine. "What does that mean?"

"I honestly have no idea. We'll hopefully know more after we have a chance to interrogate him and run his information through our databases. But that'll all have to wait until we can turn him over to local law enforcement after the hurricane passes." He glanced back toward the break room door. "For now, let's just focus on getting through the rest of the storm safely, okay?"

Nothing was truly settled between us, and we had much bigger conversations ahead. But we couldn't make any life-changing decisions while trapped in a clinic during a hurricane with a potentially dangerous criminal tied up in the next room. This fragile understanding would have to be good enough for now.

EIGHTEEN

DANIEL

I yanked open the clinic door at the first knock, squinting against the harsh morning sunlight. After the dark of the storm, the fresh-washed blue sky was almost blinding.

A thirty-something black man in a police uniform stood with his thumbs hooked in his duty belt. "You LaRue?"

"I am. You Shelton?"

"Yep."

I stepped back to let him inside. "Thanks for coming so quick. I figured I'd be bringing him in myself soon as I confirmed somebody was at the station."

Once the storm passed around six-thirty this morning, I'd radioed local PD to inform them of my captive.

"No problem." Shelton's boots squeaked against the linoleum as he followed me down the hall. "How'd our friend do overnight?"

I rolled my shoulders, sore from the fight and stiff from spending most of the night awake and on guard. "Oh, the usual insults when I tried to ask him anything. But not much more trouble he can cause from his position."

Dark circles ringed Mickey's eyes, but he looked more pissed than tired where he sat still secured to the break room chair. The moment he clapped eyes on Shelton, he tried to adopt a beleaguered expression.

"I been trying to tell them all night. I only broke in trying to get inside somewhere safe from the storm! They fucking tied me to this chair!"

"Nice try, Doyle. There are multiple witnesses who heard you attempting to break into the pharmaceutical room."

"It's a fucking conspiracy," he insisted. "You and that little doctor have it out for me."

'That little doctor' was in another room, already communicating with the triage group at the community center by radio. She'd gotten barely more sleep than I had, and courtesy of our unwelcome guest, we hadn't exactly come to a clear resolution about us.

Shelton got Mickey cuffed and on his feet. "Let's go, buddy. We've got a nice dry cell waiting for you."

"I need to take a piss."

"You can do that at the station. Come on."

I followed them back down the hall to the back door. "The task force is gonna want to speak with him."

Shelton met my gaze and nodded. "Understood."

I watched them head out into the debris-scattered street, Mickey still protesting his innocence. The storm had passed, but something told me this was just the beginning of the trouble heading for Hatterwick.

I'd need to check in with the rest of my team. By now, they were probably already scattering to help clear roads and do whatever else was needed in the wake of the hurricane. But it could wait another few minutes.

I found Gabi in her office, setting down the radio handset. Her dark hair spilled mostly around her shoulders, save for the hair elastic hanging onto the last two inches, and exhaustion lined her face. She was still beautiful, though.

"Mickey's on his way to lockup."

She nodded, rubbing her temples. "Good. The community center's got their triage running smooth. No major injuries reported yet."

"Yet being the operative word." I leaned against her doorframe. "As roads get cleared, people'll start venturing out to check their properties."

"Mm." She straightened some papers on her desk, not quite meeting my eyes. The awkwardness from our unfinished conversation last night hung between us.

"Want to do a damage assessment? Get ahead of what we might be dealing with?" We were both people of action. She'd feel better if she were doing something.

"Yeah. That's probably smart." She pulled the elastic out of her hair and shook it out before gathering the thick mass of it back into a ponytail and securing it again.

I followed Gabi out into the aftermath. The air held that particular post-hurricane stillness—heavy, humid, waiting. Debris littered Main Street like a giant had shaken out his junk drawer. Palm fronds, branches, and bits of metal roofing scattered across wet pavement. The salty breeze carried that distinctive post-storm smell—wet vegetation, disturbed earth, and something metallic.

"Could've been worse." I scanned the damage. The roofs of most buildings were intact, though Hook, Line, and Sinker's front window hadn't survived. A massive oak lay across the remains of the fence at the Methodist church, but missed the building itself.

"July storms usually are. It's the September ones you really have to watch out for." She stepped over a tangle of Spanish moss. "Power's still out everywhere else, though. Probably will be for a few days at least."

A couple of teenagers were gathered around the fallen oak, phones out to document the destruction. From further up the road, chainsaws started up as someone worked to begin to clear a path. We continued our meandering exploration toward the marina for another couple of blocks, until we found our path blocked by a massive water oak sprawled across the road, its root ball torn free of the saturated ground.

"Looks like we're not getting through there. Want to cut over to the sound side?"

Gabi nodded, already turning down the side street. Her sneakers crunched over scattered pine needles and chunks of bark. I matched her stride, keeping an eye on loose debris that might still come down. The wind had died, but damaged trees were unstable after storms.

The beach access path opened up ahead of us. Past the dunes, the sound churned gray-brown, still agitated from the storm. White-capped waves slapped against the shore—unusual for this typically calm side of the island.

We picked our way along the debris-strewn beach. Pieces of dock floated in the shallows. Torn fishing nets tangled with marsh grass. A plastic cooler lid stood partly embedded in the sand. Someone's deck chair had been twisted into an almost unrecognizable knot.

I stopped short. "Hey. You see that?"

Half-buried in wet sand at the water's edge lay the bow section of what looked like a small fishing boat, perhaps twenty feet long. Even from here, I saw splintered edges where it had broken apart.

"Think someone's boat broke loose from its moorings during the storm?" Gabi asked.

"Maybe."

Waves lapped at my boots as I circled around to the back of the wreck. The splintered edges of the bow showed fresh damage. This definitely hadn't been sitting here long. Sand was already filling the exposed cabin space, but I made out built-in storage lockers and what remained of a small berth.

The break wasn't clean. The back half had been torn away violently, probably by the force of the waves during the storm. No signs of blood or bodies, which was good. But something about this wreck nagged at me. The storage spaces looked custom-built in a way that wasn't consistent with a craft of this age. Someone might have renovated the craft. Or it might be something else.

"Daniel!" Gabi's voice carried over the sound of the waves. She stood about thirty yards down the beach, crouched near some debris tangled in marsh grass.

I picked my way across the wet sand to where she waited. As I got closer, I saw what had caught her attention—a rectangular white package wrapped in heavy clear plastic, around a foot long and four inches thick. The kind of professional-grade waterproof packaging used by drug runners.

My jaw tightened. Even partially buried in sand, there was no mistaking what it was. Pure, uncut cocaine. Worth tens of thousands on the street.

"Don't touch it," I said, though Gabi had already backed away.

I pulled my radio from my belt, keeping one eye on the package half-buried in the sand. "Echo Two-Seven, this is LaRue. Need immediate assistance about one click north of the marina on the sound side. Evidence recovery situation."

"Copy that," Vance's voice crackled back. "En route. Five minutes."

"Make it three." I scanned the beach in both directions. No

movement except waves and wind-blown debris. "We'll need additional units to secure at least a quarter-mile perimeter."

"Understood."

I clicked off and turned to Gabi. "You should head back to the clinic."

She crossed her arms. "I'm already here. I can help."

"You've helped enough finding this. But now it's an active crime scene." I kept my voice gentle but firm. "And if whoever was running these drugs is still around, I don't want them getting a look at you and thinking you can do anything to help recover their product."

"Fine." She backed further away from the package. "But come by the community center later to check in. Please."

I saw her uncertainty. The assumption that my job was going to take over everything again. I'd just have to do everything possible to show she was a priority, no matter what happened with the investigation.

"Yes, ma'am."

The distant rumble of engines grew steadily louder from the north end of the beach, cutting through the constant crash of waves against the shore. Two ATVs appeared around the rocky outcropping, their riders navigating carefully around the storm debris scattered across the sand. Rawlings and Martinez brought their vehicles to a stop about twenty feet from where I stood, engines sputtering to silence as they dismounted. Both men were already pulling evidence collection gear from the reinforced cargo boxes mounted behind their seats—cameras, measuring equipment, evidence bags, and marking flags.

Martinez straightened up, adjusting his tactical vest as he surveyed the scene before us. His dark eyes took in the damaged package, the scattered debris, and the general chaos in the wake of the storm. "Found more than storm damage, huh?"

"Yeah. And there's a wrecked boat about thirty yards that

way that needs processing too." I pointed south along the curve of the beach, where pieces of fiberglass and metal glinted in the morning sun. "Looks custom-modified. Could be our transport vessel."

Rawlings nodded grimly, already pulling on a pair of latex gloves. His weathered face was set in a focused expression. "Peterson is coordinating with local PD to get help securing the perimeter. Might take a bit though. It's not a big department."

I wasn't surprised by that assessment. Sutter's Ferry Police Department probably had maybe a dozen officers total, and half of them were likely dealing with storm cleanup and emergency calls across the island. "Figured as much. What about Vance?"

"Helping clear the main road into town. Tree came down across the intersection near the marina. He'll be along shortly once they get that sorted."

I watched as Martinez began systematically photographing the package and the surrounding area, his camera clicking steadily as he documented the scene from multiple angles. The incoming tide was my biggest concern now—we had perhaps an hour before the water reached the evidence, and possibly less if the swells kept building. "Let's work fast before the tide comes in much further. And keep your eyes open—whoever dumped this cargo might still be around looking to recover it. I'm gonna notify Hayes, then I'll join you."

I moved several yards away from the evidence collection team, close enough to keep them in sight but far enough to ensure privacy for the call. Pulling out my satellite phone, I checked the signal strength. The regular cell networks were still down after the storm, but this military-grade equipment would get through to headquarters regardless of local infrastructure damage.

The phone rang twice before a familiar voice answered. "Hayes."

"Sir, LaRue here. We've got a situation developing on Hatterwick Island."

"Go ahead."

I filled him in on everything. Hayes listened without interruption, though I heard him tapping something against his desk, as he did when processing complex information.

He was silent for a long moment after I finished my report. "That break-in at the clinic last night. You think it's connected to what you found this morning?"

"Don't know for certain yet, sir. But the guy we caught, Mickey Doyle? He was already in our task force files. He's got multiple priors for possession with intent to distribute. Local PD has him in lockup right now, awaiting interrogation."

"Alright. Document everything you find out there. I'll send Bradley's team down from Norfolk to assist with evidence collection and run an expanded beach sweep. The storm might have washed up more than just one package. And Daniel? Make sure you get in on that interrogation with the local police. Could be our first real break in this trafficking network."

"Yes, sir. Will do."

I ended the call and headed back toward the wreckage site. Martinez had already tagged and bagged the damaged package, sealing it in a waterproof evidence container that would preserve whatever remained of the contents. Meanwhile, Rawlings was methodically photographing the splintered remains of the craft.

The tide was creeping steadily higher now, foamy waves lapping at the orange evidence markers they'd placed in the sand to mark the debris field. Each wave erased a little more of the storm's revelations. We had a lot of ground to cover before the water erased whatever other evidence the hurricane had exposed along this stretch of coastline. But after months of dead ends and false leads, we finally had concrete proof of active trafficking operations on Hatterwick Island. Now we just had to figure out who was running the network and how deep their operation went into the island's community.

I pulled on a fresh pair of gloves and grabbed an evidence bag from the kit. Time to get to work and see what other secrets the storm had decided to give up.

NINETEEN

GABI

The community center parking lot was already mostly full when I arrived, emergency vehicles and civilian cars crowded haphazardly near the entrance like scattered puzzle pieces. The hurricane's aftermath had drawn what looked like half the island here—some arriving to offer help, others desperately seeking it. I recognized old Mr. Henderson's rusted Chevy next to the Monteros' sedan, both families probably dealing with their own storm damage but still showing up to pitch in. That was Hatterwick for you—when disaster struck, the community pulled together.

Inside, folding tables lined the walls, stacked with medical supplies and bottled water. The basketball court had transformed into a makeshift triage area, complete with rows of cots and privacy screens. The squeak of sneakers on polished wood mixed with urgent voices and the clatter of equipment.

Justin waved from where he was setting up an IV stand. "Over here, Doc!"

Kristie intercepted me before I reached him. "Thank God you're here. We've got mostly minor injuries—cuts from debris cleanup, a couple of sprains. Mrs. Jackson's blood pressure is through the roof again."

A group of volunteers hauled in more supplies through the side entrance, directed by the emergency management team. Some faces I recognized from the clinic; others were residents I'd treated over the past couple of months. Plenty more I'd simply known all my life. The familiar rhythm of controlled chaos settled over me—not unlike a busy ER shift, just with a distinct island flavor.

I scanned the setup, mentally cataloging what we had and what we still needed. The basic triage stations looked solid, but we'd need to establish a better flow for incoming patients. The mess of vehicles outside would impede any serious emergencies from being able to easily get inside. And someone would have to coordinate with the pharmacy about prescription refills for people who'd lost medications.

I snagged Curtis Bowen, one of the EMT firefighters, and tasked him with sorting out the parking lot. Then I crossed the room to check in with Justin.

I recognized the grizzled old man on the cot. "Mr. Collins, what's going on with you this morning?"

The elderly fisherman flashed a shaky smile. "Just wanted to check my ticker after all that excitement. Storm had me wound up something fierce."

I thought of the less than restful night I'd spent at the clinic with Daniel and our captive. "It did that for all of us. Deep breath in for me." I pressed the stethoscope against his chest. "And out slowly."

After I'd listened, I eased back, checking the vitals Justin had already gathered. "Your heart sounds good. Blood pressure's a bit elevated, but that's expected. How's that hip doing?"

"Better since you adjusted my meds last month. Sarah says I'm not grumbling near as much."

"Glad to hear it." My brain flipped through the mental list of patients I'd seen, wondering if I knew her. It finally registered that Sarah was his granddaughter. Newly pregnant. She'd been the one to bring him in for his last appointment. "Speaking of Sarah, is she keeping up with her prenatal vitamins?"

His weathered face broke into a proud grandfather's smile. "Sure is. That great-grandbaby's due right around Christmas."

I moved on to Jenny Reyes, who'd sliced her palm, helping clear branches from her yard. As I cleaned and bandaged the wound, she updated me on her son's college applications.

"—apply for that scholarship I told you about?" I tied off the gauze. "The one for children of commercial fishermen?"

"First thing Monday. Thanks again for telling us about it."

"Of course." It had been scholarships that had paid for my education off island. I knew the challenges a lot of people here had in finding ways to pay for college that didn't involve taking out student loans that wouldn't be paid off until retirement.

Mrs. Jackson was next, her usually immaculate silver hair disheveled from the night's stress. Her blood pressure had indeed spiked, but fifteen minutes of quiet conversation about her grandchildren's recent visit brought it down to more reasonable levels.

Between patients, I caught snippets of storm damage reports—mostly minor flooding and debris, though the pier had taken a beating. At least two boats had broken free of their ties at the marina and were unaccounted for. Half a dozen more were floating in the harbor, and a team was being dispatched to retrieve them. Quite a few folks had lost their stairs down to the beach, and there were missing chunks of roofs all over the island, but it could have been so much worse. The collective relief was palpable.

"Doc?" Justin appeared at my elbow. "Got a sprained ankle over here. Teenager who thought aftermath cleanup was a good time for parkour."

I suppressed a smile, already knowing which of our local daredevils it would be. Sure enough, Tommy Jensen sat sheepishly on the exam table, his mother standing nearby with her arms crossed.

"So, Tommy," I pulled up a rolling stool. "Want to tell me what happened, or should I guess based on your last two visits?"

I listened to him describing the incident while his poor mom grimaced. I shot her a sympathetic smile. "Tim's pyrotechnics are seeming pretty same now, aren't they?" Tommy's elder brother, grown now, had been on the receiving end of plenty of lectures from Hoyt and the rest of his crew over his teen years. His failed cannon experiment still got talked about from time to time.

Mrs. Jensen groaned. "Don't remind me."

Holding in a smile, I turned to Tommy. "Next time you decide to practice your stunts, maybe wait until after we've cleared all the debris? Your poor mom needs a break." I finished wrapping Tommy's ankle and handed his mother an ice pack. "Twenty minutes on, twenty off. And stay off it as much as possible for the next few days."

"Gabi!" Caroline's voice cut through the organized chaos of the community center, sharp with the particular brand of exhaustion that only comes from managing two energetic kids during a crisis. My sister threaded her way between the cots, dodging volunteers carrying supplies and patients waiting for treatment, her movements quick and purposeful despite the fatigue etched in the lines around her eyes.

I met her halfway across the crowded space, pulling her into a quick hug that smelled of coffee and the faint saltiness that seemed to cling to everything after a storm. "Everything okay at home?"

"The kids are driving me up the wall." Her voice carried that frayed edge every parent gets when they've reached their limit. "They've been cooped up too long, and you know how they get." She smoothed back a few wisps of dark hair that had escaped her ponytail, the gesture automatic and telling. "Logan's convinced he's going to find buried treasure in all the mess the storm washed up on the beach, and Aubrey keeps trying to sneak out to help him. I swear, if I have to chase them down one more time today..."

"Sounds about right for those two." I didn't bother suppressing a smile at the mental image of my nephew and niece embarking on their post-hurricane adventure. I grabbed a bottle of water from a nearby table laden with donated refreshments and handed it to her. "Have you been home yet? House make it through okay?"

"Lost a few shingles off the back roof, but nothing major. Thank God for small mercies." She twisted the cap off the water bottle, her movements sharp with lingering stress. "Hoyt's been out since dawn with the emergency crews. They're focusing on Shore Drive first, trying to clear the main routes. Apparently, the surge took out a big section of the road where it curves around the inlet."

That was the road leading to the north end of the island, where Willa and Sawyer had weathered the storm at the historic Sutter House. The knowledge sent a small spike of worry through me. "You heard anything from Willa or Sawyer?"

"No, but cell towers are still down across most of the island. I'm sure they're fine, though." She took a long drink, then wiped her mouth with the back of her hand. "You know that old house has survived worse storms than this one. The Wilsons lost their entire deck though, and that old boat shed by the marina finally collapsed. Been threatening to do that for years. Could've been much worse, all things considered."

Caroline glanced around the bustling community center, taking in the controlled chaos of triage stations, volunteer coordination tables, and the steady stream of islanders seeking medical attention for storm-related injuries. "Need any help here? I can pitch in for a few hours before the kids drive poor Ibbie completely insane. She's been a saint watching them, but even saints have their limits."

"We've got it covered for now. The team here are absolute rock stars." I nodded toward where patients with minor injuries were being efficiently processed by the EMTs and my nurses, their movements choreographed by years of working together in crisis situations. "Go home. Keep my niece and nephew from becoming amateur treasure hunters. Or at least make sure they wear shoes while they're digging through storm debris. Last thing we need is them showing up here with puncture wounds."

Caroline laughed, the first genuine smile I'd seen from her all morning. "Don't give them any ideas. They're creative enough on their own."

The rest of the morning devolved into a blur of familiar faces marked by scrapes, bruises, and the occasional deeper cut from cleanup efforts gone wrong. Thankfully, none of the injuries required medical evacuation to the mainland or anything requiring emergency hospitalization.

Ed Cartwright's distinctive grumbling reached me before I actually saw him, his booming voice carrying across the community center's high-ceilinged space as Bree guided him toward one of the treatment areas with the patient persistence of someone who'd been managing stubborn men her entire life.

"It's just a scratch, Pop," Bree insisted, her tone caught somewhere between exasperation and genuine concern. "Let the doctor look at it properly."

"Damn fool thing to do, trying to clear that branch myself," Ed muttered, settling his considerable frame onto the exam chair with a grunt of resignation. He held a blood-spotted dish towel against his forearm, the white fabric already stained rust-red. "Should've waited for help, but you know how I get when there's work to be done."

I pulled on a fresh pair of latex gloves. "Let me see what we're dealing with here, Ed."

The cut wasn't particularly deep, but it was jagged enough to need proper cleaning and care—the kind of wound that came from tangling with storm debris and losing. As I worked, cleaning the wound with gentle but thorough strokes, Ed updated me on the storm's impact across the island with the authority of someone who'd lived through dozens of these events.

"Lost three windows at the brewery," he said, his voice tight as I dabbed antiseptic along the cut. "Water got in before we got them boarded back up properly. Made a real mess of the front room."

"The equipment's all fine, and the structural damage is minimal," Bree interjected, her hand resting protectively on her grandfather's shoulder. "We'll need to replace some drywall and possibly refinish the floors, but insurance should cover most of it."

I carefully placed the first butterfly bandage, holding the wound edges together. "Any word from Willa and Sawyer? I know they rode out the storm at Sutter House, but with the cell towers down..."

"Nothing yet," Bree admitted. "But that house was built to handle storms far worse than this one. It's survived everything the Atlantic's thrown at it for close to two centuries. I'm sure they're fine, just waiting for the roads to clear enough for them to get back to town."

Ed winced slightly as I applied pressure to secure another bandage. "That girl picked a hell of a time for her extended honeymoon period, I'll give her that. Though I suppose Mother Nature doesn't consult anyone's calendar."

"There." I smoothed the last bandage into place and stepped back to examine my handiwork. "Keep it clean and dry for the next few days. Come by the clinic later this week so I can check how it's healing and change the dressing."

"Thanks, Doc." Ed flexed his arm carefully, testing the range of motion. "Feels better already. Now if you'll excuse me, I've got a date with a chainsaw and what remains of my poor oak tree. That old beauty's been blocking my driveway since about three this morning."

"Pop, absolutely not." Bree's tone carried the kind of authority that brooked no argument. "You're going straight home to rest that arm. I'll call the tree service first thing."

"Ain't no formal tree service gonna be operating normally on this island for at least a couple of weeks," Ed protested, though his voice lacked real conviction. "Half their equipment's probably damaged, and the other half's gonna be tied up with emergency calls."

The sound of their familiar bickering gradually faded as they made their way toward the exit, Ed's grumbling punctuated by Bree's patient but firm responses—a dance they'd been performing for years.

I sat back against the treatment table, allowing myself a moment to pause and chug down an entire bottle of water. The cool liquid felt like heaven against my parched throat. They were probably right about Willa and Sawyer being fine. Sutter House had weathered countless storms over the centuries, and if anyone could handle being temporarily cut off from civilization, it was those two. I was just feeling antsy not being able to confirm the safety of one of my people, the way any good doctor worries about their community.

Shrugging off the lingering sense of disquiet that seemed to follow every natural disaster, I tossed the empty water bottle into the recycling bin and went back to work.

By early afternoon, we still hadn't found the stern of the drug runner's vessel. But the scene had been secured. Additional parcels had been recovered along the beach as far as two miles up the length of the island. A team would remain in place for a while, as we expected more to turn up with the changing of the tides. Hopefully, some part of the boat with the HIN or other identifier would be found and give us a lead on who the boat actually belonged to. Given the evidence we had, it was unclear whether the drug runners had actually been attempting to make a run during the hurricane, or if the vessel had gotten loose and damaged. We might never know for sure, unless a body or an owner turned up to connect to it.

I'd handed over incident command to Bradley so I could get to the Sutter's Ferry Police Station for Mickey Doyle's interrogation. Maybe he'd have more light to shed on the situation. Assuming we motivated him to talk.

Police Chief Bill Carson was waiting for me. A weathered guy who might've been anywhere from fifty to late sixties, his face was set in lines of grim irritation. "Shame this asshole couldn't have waited for a better time to do this. We got bigger things to worry about after this hurricane than the likes of some opportunistic tweaker."

That attitude was likely what had allowed Doyle to make it this far. But I knew my role here. "That's the damned truth. But our intelligence suggests he may be more than that. I'd appreciate it if you'd let me assist with the interrogation."

He fixed me with a narrow-eyed glare. "You one of Hayes'?"

"Yes, sir."

He nodded. "Reckon you can be there, then. But let me take the lead."

"Understood."

I followed him into the interrogation room. Mickey was already seated at the lone table, his hands cuffed to the table. Given his extreme look of boredom and annoyance, I wondered how long he'd been there. I didn't expect this station to have much in the way of holding facilities. Probably not more than a couple of cells.

Mickey's eyes fixed on me, his expression darkening. "You again."

Carson settled into the chair across from Mickey. His weathered hands folded on the scratched metal table, and when he spoke, his voice carried the weight of decades in law enforcement. "So. You want to tell me what you were doing at the clinic during a hurricane?"

Mickey slouched deeper in his seat, the metal chair creaking under his weight. His clothes were still damp from the storm, and he smelled like wet concrete and desperation. "Man, I was just looking for shelter from the storm."

I remained standing against the concrete block wall, arms crossed, studying his body language. The guy was nervous—leg bouncing, eyes darting everywhere except at us. "By jimmying the back door?"

"Look, I ain't talking to you, Coast Guard." Mickey's voice carried a defiant edge, but I heard the underlying tremor of fear.

Carson's weathered face cracked into something that might have been a smile if you squinted, but looked more like the expression a shark makes before it bites. "Son, you're already looking at breaking and entering during a state of emergency. That's a felony in North Carolina. Add attempted theft of controlled substances, plus this handy list of outstanding warrants we've got for you on other drug charges from three different counties, and you're facing some serious time. We're talking fifteen to twenty years if you draw the wrong judge."

Mickey's face went pale, the color draining out of his cheeks like someone had pulled a plug. "How'd you—"

"We found your previous attempts to get in. Left some nice prints on the door frame and window sill. Real considerate of you." Carson's tone remained conversational, almost friendly.

"Can't prove that was from before and not last night."

"Doesn't matter." I pushed off the wall, taking a step closer to the table. "We both heard you muttering to yourself when you figured out you couldn't get into the drug room without the power being up. Your bosses know you're this sloppy?"

Mickey's shoulders hunched like he was trying to make himself smaller. His cuffed hands twisted against the metal restraints. "They ain't my bosses no more."

"No?" Carson's voice stayed casual, but I caught the sharp interest in his eyes. "What happened there?"

Mickey's leg bounced faster under the table, his gaze ping-ponging between the one-way mirror, the ceiling tiles, the corner of the room—anywhere but at us. The silence stretched out for nearly a minute before he finally cracked. "Lost a shipment. Twenty-five grand worth. They said I had to pay it back."

"By when?" I kept my tone neutral.

"End of the month." He swallowed hard, his Adam's apple bobbing. "Hurricane was coming. Figured everyone would be distracted or evacuated. Clinic's got painkillers, other stuff I could sell fast. OxyContin, Percocet, maybe some Adderall. Would've covered most of what I owed."

Carson leaned forward slightly, his elbows on the table. "And who exactly were you planning to sell to?"

"Same guys I owed. Figured they'd take it as payment and give me another chance." Mickey's laugh was hollow and bitter. "Stupid plan, right? But I was desperate. They ain't the forgiving type. You don't pay what you owe, bad things happen. Real bad things."

So the break-in wasn't directly related to the trafficking operation we were investigating. It really had been a crime of opportunity, born from desperation and poor judgment. That made me feel a little bit better about the whole situation. Gabi hadn't been targeted specifically, and the clinic itself would probably be fine going forward.

But that didn't mean this was all Mickey knew. A guy like him, running product for organized dealers, had to have picked up useful intelligence along the way.

Carson apparently had the same thought. He drummed his fingers on the table in a slow, methodical rhythm. "Seeing as you're not getting back in with them, doesn't seem like you owe them much allegiance anymore. You could trade information for a reduced sentence. You give us something useful about their operation, we help you out with the DA. Get those charges knocked down to simple B&E, time served."

"Information like what?" Mickey's voice was cautious now, calculating.

"What can you tell us about your bosses' operation?" I moved to lean against the wall where he could see me clearly. "How big is it? Who's running it? How does the product move?"

Mickey's eyes darted between Carson and me, weighing his options. I practically saw the gears turning in his head—fear of his former associates versus the very real prospect of serious prison time. Finally, he slumped further in his chair, resignation settling over his features like a heavy blanket.

"Started with the Lowe brothers about two years ago. They got me running small packages up and down the coast. Nothing major at first—an ounce or two of blow, some pills. Then they introduced me to Heneghan. Big Irish guy, arms like tree trunks. He's the one handles most of the local distribution—splitting bigger shipments into smaller ones, getting them out to street dealers."

Carson made a note on his pad. "And Ortiz?"

"Man, I never met him, and I don't want to." Mickey shuddered visibly. "That son of a bitch is scary as hell. Shows up every couple of months to check on things, make sure nobody's skimming. Works with some guy they call the Skipper—he's the one who actually moves most of the product around the coast. Then there's this dude, the Shell Man, who handles the money side of things."

I kept my expression carefully neutral. Code names weren't surprising in an operation like this, and while they weren't immediately helpful for identification, they gave us a clearer picture of the organizational structure. "Where do they usually make the transfers?"

"Changes all the time. Security, you know? Sometimes it's the old fish processing plant down in Wilmington. Other times they use these fishing boats—make it look like they're just bringing in the day's catch. There are a couple of marinas they like, places where the Coast Guard doesn't patrol as heavy."

"How much product are we talking about?" Carson asked.

Mickey shrugged, the metal cuffs clinking against the table. "Used to be twenty, thirty grand worth per run when I started. Now? Man, last month they moved half a million through here in one go. Big white bricks of powder, pills by the thousands."

Half a million dollars. That was significantly more than the task force's initial estimates suggested. This operation was bigger and more sophisticated than we'd thought, which meant it was also more dangerous.

"And where exactly are they storing all this before distribution?" Carson's tone stayed casual, but I watched his interest sharpen like a blade.

"Dunno for sure. I wasn't involved in any of that upper-level stuff. Seems like it probably moves around for security. But lately there's been talk about setting up something more permanent. Something about having protection from higher up, whatever that means."

That last bit made my blood run cold. Protection from higher up might mean corrupted local officials, possibly even federal agents. It definitely bore further investigation, and it meant this case was about to get a lot more complicated.

Carson and I continued the interrogation for another twenty minutes, but it became clear that Mickey's knowledge had limits. He knew nothing about the top-level organizers or the financial structure of the organization. The full scope of the operation was beyond his pay grade. I was pretty sure we were nearly done extracting useful information.

"One more thing." I straightened up from the wall. "You know anything about a boat from your bosses' fleet going down in the storm?"

Mickey blinked owlishly. "Huh?"

"We found the wreckage on the sound side of the island. Fishing boat, maybe thirty-five feet. Torn more or less in half by the storm surge. We definitely recovered some product from the debris field."

Mickey whistled low. "Ooo, they'll be pissed about that. Losing product is bad for business. But naw, I don't know nothing about somebody trying to make a run *during* the hurricane. That's crazy talk, even for these guys."

Carson glanced at me with raised eyebrows, but I was through with my questions. The interrogation had yielded more than I'd expected, but we'd hit the limits of what Mickey could tell us. Carson gestured toward the one-way mirror, and a moment later Officer Shelton came inside to uncuff Mickey from the table and escort him back to a holding cell.

"Wait, what kinda deal am I gonna get?" Mickey's voice rose with panic as Shelton helped him to his feet.

"That'll depend on the district attorney," Carson informed him. "We can't even get in touch with her until the phones are back up and the roads are clear. Until then, you're cooling your jets in a cell. Might want to use the time to think about what else you might remember."

Mickey was still grumbling and protesting as Shelton escorted him down the narrow hallway toward the holding area.

Carson scrubbed a hand over his weathered face, the lines around his eyes deepening with fatigue. "Like we needed more problems for this island. Did you get what you needed?"

"Got as much as I think we were gonna get out of him." I stretched, working out the kinks from standing against the wall. "Anything he said flag for you or connect to other criminal activity you've seen on the island?"

"No, not really." Carson shook his head slowly. "Your task force has been in touch before asking about the same kind of thing, but mostly things have been quiet here. There's always some drug stuff that comes up during tourist season—kids from the mainland bringing party favors, locals selling a little weed to make ends meet. But mostly it seems to be coming from off-island. Marijuana, some harder party shit like molly and coke. If Hatterwick is being used as a drop point for anything more serious than that, it's the first I'm hearing of it." His expression darkened. "I don't like it. I don't like it one damned bit."

Neither did I. The idea of a major trafficking operation using this small, close-knit community as a waystation was deeply troubling. But I was reasonably sure Hayes would consider Mickey's information sufficiently credible intelligence to establish a more permanent Coast Guard presence on Hatterwick for further investigation. If I had my way, I'd volunteer to be part of that operation.

Carson and I stepped out of the interrogation room into the main area of the small police station. The building felt cramped and understaffed, probably designed for handling minor tourist infractions and domestic disputes rather than major criminal investigations. I spotted Officer Shelton in the bullpen, just hanging up an old-fashioned radio handset.

"Chief, Teague radioed in from the north end," Shelton called out. "He confirmed that Willa Sutter did actually find human remains on her property."

"Well, fuck," Carson spat, his face immediately shifting into a harder expression.

My focus sharpened instinctively. "Human remains? Where exactly?" My first thought was the missing pilot from the drug boat that had washed up on the sound side. Perhaps the body had been carried around the island by the storm surge.

"North end of the island. Atlantic side, up near the old lighthouse." Shelton's expression was grim. "He said it looks like they've been there for a while. Skeletal remains, mostly. Probably got uncovered or displaced by the storm."

Not the missing boat pilot, then. These remains had been there much longer than a few days.

Carson went still, his face losing a shade or two of color. When he spoke, his voice was tight with an emotion I couldn't quite identify. "We need to get out there. Now."

Shelton's own face was grave as he nodded. "You think it might be—"

"We don't know what it could be," Carson cut him off sharply. "But we do this by the fucking book in case it is what we're thinking."

I sensed undercurrents I didn't understand, some piece of local history or knowledge that I wasn't privy to. "Can I offer my help? Coast Guard has experience with recovery operations."

Carson shook his head firmly. "This is island business, LaRue. You've done enough for one day."

It seemed I was being dismissed. I recognized the closing of ranks when I saw it, and I had enough of my own responsibilities to deal with. The storm damage assessment was still ongoing, and I needed to check in with my commanding officer about the drug boat recovery and Mickey's intelligence. But as I made my way out of the cramped police station and into the humid afternoon air, something about the encounter kept circling in my brain like a persistent fly.

Something about the name of the woman who'd found the remains. Willa? Why was that familiar?

It wasn't until I'd made it half a block down the debris-strewn street, stepping around a fallen power line and what looked like half of somebody's roof, that the connection clicked into place. One of Gabi's close friends was named Willa. I'd heard her mention the name several times over the months we'd been seeing each other.

And it sounded like this Willa had just stumbled upon a whole different kind of trouble than a simple drug bust.

TWENTY-ONE

GABI

I rubbed my tired eyes, finally allowing myself to feel the bone-deep exhaustion from the past twenty-four hours. The stream of patients had slowed to a trickle as afternoon crept in. Most injuries had been minor—cuts, sprains, one broken arm from someone who'd slipped off a roof trying to determine how bad the damage was from a tree that had fallen on his house. He'd been lucky that was the only thing that had broken. We'd handled it all without a problem, and I was so beyond grateful for the nurses and EMTs, and for the retired GP on vacation who'd showed up to volunteer his services this morning.

Through the community center windows, I watched crews clearing fallen trees from the roads. The hum of chainsaws had become background noise. Word was that power would be restored to most of the island by nightfall, which was a minor miracle.

"Dr. Carrera, why don't you take a break?" Betty Jo Freeman, one of our nurses, touched my arm. "We can handle things for a while."

I nodded, realizing I hadn't eaten since the protein bar I'd scarfed down at dawn. My legs felt wobbly as I stood, and that's when I saw him. Daniel moved through the crowd with purpose, his Coast Guard uniform muddy and wrinkled. My heart did that familiar stutter of surprise and joy. I still wasn't used to seeing him here on Hatterwick. I wasn't used to seeing him anymore at all.

But something was off. His jaw was set, brows drawn together in that way that meant serious business. My stomach clenched. Had they found something in the wreckage of that boat? Was he being called away already? Damn it, I wasn't ready to say goodbye to him again. Not with everything still so unsettled between us.

He caught my eye across the room and picked up his pace. The determined expression on his face made my pulse race as he approached. Whatever news he carried, it was clear this wasn't going to be a casual conversation.

"Hey." His voice was low, urgent. "Can you get away for a bit?"

My stomach dropped. "Betty Jo, I'm taking fifteen."

She waved me off without looking up from her charts.

Daniel led me down the hall to an empty classroom that had clearly been used for kids' summer programming. The walls were covered in children's artwork, bright crayon drawings a stark contrast to his grim expression.

"What's going on?"

"Willa Sutter. She a friend of yours?"

Hers was perhaps the last name I expected to hear from his lips. Ice spread through my chest. "Yes. Is she hurt? What's wrong?"

"I don't think she's hurt. But, well, while I was at the police station, they were talking about how she found some human remains on her property."

The room tilted slightly. I gripped the edge of a table to

steady myself. "Remains?" The word came out as barely more than a whisper. With Daniel's training, if it had been a fresh body, he'd have said that. Which meant...

"Not quite sure. Atlantic side of the island. Somewhere further north. The police are trying to get more than one officer out there."

Oh God. After all these years, had they finally found Gwen? My heart pounded against my ribs.

"Gabs, are you okay?"

I shook my head, trying to clear it. "I need to get to Willa."

"Come on. I've got a boat." He didn't hesitate, didn't ask questions. Just offered exactly what I needed, and my chest tightened with gratitude even through the rising sense of panic and dread.

The wind whipped my hair as Daniel gunned the Zodiac's engine, sending us skimming across the choppy water. I gripped the rope that ran along the side of the boat, knuckles white. The smell of diesel and salt water filled my nose as we curved past the southern tip of the island. Up ahead, I could see the decommissioned lighthouse that had once guided vessels safely into the sound. The lighthouse and caretaker's cottage had been converted into a home and expanded over the years by Ford Donoghue's moms. From my vantage point on the water, it seemed they hadn't sustained any major damage from the storm surge or high winds.

"Hold on," Daniel called over the engine's roar. "It's gonna get rougher once we hit the Atlantic side."

He wasn't kidding. The moment we rounded the point, the swells grew larger, the ocean still churning from the remnants of the storm. The Zodiac bounced over each wave, salt spray stinging my face. I clutched my medical bag tighter, though I doubted its contents would be needed for what we might find.

My mind raced with possibilities. After all these years, could the storm have actually uncovered Gwen's remains?

"You want to tell me what we might be dealing with?" Daniel's voice cut through my thoughts.

I'd never mentioned this to him in all our time together. Seemed only fair to tell him now. "There used to be three of us. Me, Willa, and Gwen. BFFs forever. Then, twelve years ago, Gwen disappeared from the end of school beach party. No trace of her has ever been found."

There was so much more to it than that. But those were the essentials.

Grim sympathy flashed across Daniel's face. "You think the remains could be hers."

"I don't know." And I couldn't decide if it was better or worse if it was. Was it better to finally have conclusive answers that our friend was dead or to have the mystery remain, along with the admittedly slim hope she could be out there alive somewhere?

"Either way, Willa's likely to be in a state. She just lost her grandfather about six weeks ago, and she was the one who found him."

"Shit." Jaw set, Daniel pushed the throttle forward.

The coastline blurred past as we made our way north, the familiar landmarks of my childhood home looking alien and threatening in the storm's aftermath. And then I saw the small cluster of people at the edge of the maritime forest. As Daniel began throttling back, I picked out Sawyer's tall frame first, then Officer Teague's familiar red beard. And Willa.

My heart clenched. Even from this distance, I could see how badly she was shaking despite the foil emergency blanket wrapped around her shoulders. Her massive pit bull, Roy, pressed against her legs, providing what comfort he could.

Daniel expertly beached the boat, and I was over the side

before he'd cut the engine completely, my shoes sinking into wet sand as I rushed toward my friend.

"Oh my God, Willa! We just heard. Are you okay?"

The moment I reached her, I could see she wasn't. Not even close. Her face was ghost-white, eyes glazed and distant in that way that meant she was probably dissociating. Blood stained her knees as if she'd fallen. The emergency blanket did little to stop her violent trembling.

"I'm not hurt," she whispered.

My doctor's instincts kicked in as I assessed her condition. The bloody knees were superficial, but combined with the shock and clear trauma response, I knew she needed medical attention.

"Honey, you have blood on your knees. And if you're wrapped up in that foil blanket and still cold, you're definitely in shock. I want to get you into the clinic."

"No!" The sharp desperation in her voice made me flinch. "I just want to go home."

"Willa—" I started to protest, but Daniel's warm hand pressed against my back.

"Maybe give her a chance to breathe, Gabs. Reckon she's done had herself a bit of a scare."

The familiar drawl of his accent surprised me almost as much as his presence here. But he was right. I needed to back off, let her process. The doctor in me wanted to fix everything immediately, but sometimes being a friend meant knowing when to wait.

He turned to offer a half-smile to Sawyer. "We'll give y'all a lift somewhere, if you need."

Sawyer took the hand he offered. "That'd be good. My wife's had a hell of a day. Who are you, by the way?"

"Pardon me. Petty Officer First Class Daniel LaRue, U.S. Coast Guard. At your service."

I watched as they helped Willa into the Zodiac, my heart aching at how unsteady she was. Daniel caught her when she nearly fell, and I hurried to sit beside her once we got her settled with a life jacket. Ever the protective guardian, Roy flattened himself next to her.

I took her icy hands in mine. "I've gotcha. Headache?"

"Migraine," she gritted out.

"We'll get you fixed up as soon as we get back to Sutter House."

Willa's eyes squeezed shut against what I suspected was increasing pain, but she still managed to mutter, "New Orleans?"

I understood without further clarification what she was asking. My cheeks warmed. "Remember that situationship I mentioned?" It was all I'd had a chance to tell her when I'd first returned to Hatterwick.

"Yeah?"

"He's him. I'll explain everything later."

"Holding you to that."

Daniel fired up the motor, cutting off further conversation. The trip up to Sutter House at the northern tip of the island was mercifully quick. Once we reached the dock, the men secured the boat and helped us out.

"We'll get those knees cleaned, some meds for your migraine, and I'll finish checking you over. I've got something that will help you sleep if the migraine meds don't do it."

"No!" Willa jerked away from me, backing into Sawyer.

His arms came around her protectively. "It's okay. Nobody's gonna sedate you, Wren."

I stared at my friend, thrown by her extreme reaction. While her behavior could be explained by the trauma she'd just experienced, I sensed there was more to it. But now wasn't the time to push.

We made our way slowly up to the house, the men discussing storm damage and power restoration timelines. I noticed Willa growing more distant with each step, retreating into herself in a way that worried me deeply.

In the end, Sawyer was the one who cleaned and bandaged Willa's knees and hands with supplies from my medical bag. She remained eerily quiet, responding only in monosyllables when I examined her. The thousand-yard stare in her eyes scared me. I'd seen Willa retreat into herself before, but this was different. This was full dissociation.

"I don't like this, Sawyer. She's way too shocky." Was this all because of what she'd seen, or was something else going on?

"She'll be better after she's slept," he assured me, but I could see the worry in his eyes too.

I gave him a quick rundown of symptoms to watch for—changes in breathing, increased confusion, severe headache beyond the migraine. Basic things that might indicate she needed immediate medical attention beyond what we'd already provided. But I knew pushing for more right now would only make things worse.

Daniel hung back, giving us space while still staying close enough to help if needed. The quiet efficiency with which he'd handled everything today—from getting me to Willa quickly to helping transport her home—made my heart ache with gratitude. It was exactly the kind of thoughtfulness that had drawn me to him in the first place.

I watched Willa's eyes grow heavy as the migraine medication took effect. Part of me wanted to stay to make sure she was really okay. But I knew Sawyer would take good care of her, and my hovering wouldn't help.

What terrified me most was not knowing exactly what—or rather who—Willa had likely found out there in the maritime forest.

I'd spent years trying not to think about that night twelve years ago, about the friend who'd vanished without a trace from that beach party. But now all those memories came flooding back with startling clarity—the three of us giggling at sleepovers, sharing secrets about boys and dreams, planning our futures with the certainty that only teenagers possessed. Never imagining that one of us wouldn't make it to those futures we'd mapped out with such innocent confidence. Gwen had been so full of life, so determined to see the world beyond Hatterwick's shores. The thought that she might have been lying out there all this time, alone in the dark beneath the maritime pines...

"Ready to head home?" Daniel's quiet voice came from behind me, gentle enough not to startle but firm enough to pull me back from the spiral of dark thoughts.

I turned to find him leaning against the doorframe of Willa's bedroom, his Coast Guard uniform still covered in sand and salt spray from our search and rescue efforts. The events of the past twenty-four hours showed clearly in the deep shadows under his eyes and the stubble darkening his strong jaw. Despite his obvious exhaustion, concern for me radiated from his expression—that careful attention he always paid to my well-being that made my chest tighten with emotion I wasn't ready to name.

"Yeah." I gathered my medical bag from the nightstand, double-checking that I'd left Sawyer with enough supplies— extra migraine medication, anti-nausea tablets, and clear instructions for monitoring. "Let me just make sure I didn't forget anything."

"She's in good hands." Daniel nodded toward where Sawyer sat vigil beside the bed, his large frame folded into the antique chair he'd pulled close to Willa's side. Roy's massive black head rested heavily on Sawyer's knee, the pit bull's dark eyes never leaving his mistress's sleeping form. "And you look dead on your feet, Gabi."

He wasn't wrong. The adrenaline that had carried me through the morning's crisis was fading fast, leaving bone-deep exhaustion in its wake that made my limbs feel heavy and my thoughts sluggish. More than that, I needed space to process what this discovery might mean for all of us. If those remains belonged to Gwen, if she'd been out there all along just miles from where we'd grown up together...

I swallowed hard against the lump forming in my throat, tasting the salt of unshed tears. "Okay. Let's go."

EPILOGUE

DANIEL

In the wake of delivering Willa and Sawyer back to Sutter House, Gabi looked about ready to drop. Her shoulders sagged with exhaustion, and I could see the telltale signs of fatigue creeping in around her eyes. The adrenaline that had carried her through the day was wearing off. I wanted to take her straight home, tuck her into bed, and let her rest for the next twelve hours, but I should've known my girl would insist on checking back in at the community center first. Even dead on her feet, she wouldn't abandon her responsibilities.

Patients had thinned out since we'd left, but there were still some lingering cases being handled by the skeleton crew that remained. The worst of the post-hurricane medical emergencies had been dealt with, leaving mostly minor cuts, bruises, and exhaustion-related issues. She left me at the door to go touch base with the EMTs and nursing staff still running things, her professional mask sliding back into place as she moved through the organized chaos with practiced efficiency.

I stepped away from the bustle, finding a quiet corner near

the supply closets to make the call I'd been putting off. The scent of antiseptic and bleach hung heavy in the air, mixing with the lingering dampness from the storm. I pulled out my phone and dialed Hayes, knowing he'd be waiting for an update on today's developments.

"What's the status, LaRue?"

I filled him in on Mickey Doyle's interrogation, keeping my voice low to avoid being overheard by any civilians nearby. "He folded pretty quick once we had him cornered. Gave up some names—mostly street-level dealers we already knew about—small fish who've been on our radar for months. Middle management of the organization seems to be using code names exclusively, so he had nothing but aliases to report. But reading between the lines, sir, I think there's more happening here than he knows about. This feels like the tip of the iceberg."

Hayes grunted in agreement on the other end of the line, and I could hear him shuffling papers in the background. "My thoughts exactly. What's your assessment of the situation?"

"My recommendation would be to embed some operatives in Sutter's Ferry long term. Get eyes on the ground, build relationships with the locals, gather intelligence the old-fashioned way." I sucked in a breath and took the shot I'd been planning since the moment Hayes first mentioned this assignment. "Full disclosure, sir—the woman I'm involved with is here on Hatterwick. I'm going to be here during my personal time anyway, so I volunteer to be one of those embedded operatives. I'll understand if you think it's a conflict of interest."

There was a long pause, and I could almost hear the wheels turning in Hayes's head as he weighed the pros and cons. Then he chuckled, a dry sound that held more amusement than I'd expected. "You work fast, LaRue."

"It was a pre-existing relationship, sir. I'm just here to fix what I broke." The admission came easier than I'd thought it would. "I messed up with her before by letting the job take priority. I'm hoping this assignment might give me a chance to prove I've learned from that mistake."

"Well, seems like killing two birds with one stone to me, LaRue. So long as you don't let your personal feelings interfere with the job or compromise the investigation in any way."

"Absolutely not, sir. I can maintain complete professionalism during operations while using my downtime to rebuild my relationship." The relief in my voice was obvious, but I didn't care.

"Good. Any thoughts on who else would suit this kind of long-term operation?"

The question caught me off guard. Hayes asking for my input on personnel decisions wasn't something I'd expected, especially not this early in my posting. "You're asking me, sir?"

"You've shown good instincts throughout this case. Done solid work under pressure. I value your assessment." The praise was matter-of-fact, but it hit me like a physical blow.

The unexpected validation had my chest warming with pride. I ran through what I knew about our team and the specifics of this investigation. "Well, sir, with Doyle implicating the commercial fishing industry as a major component of the smuggling operation, we want somebody who can integrate into that sector without raising suspicion. If I remember correctly from the personnel files, O'Connell is from Hatterwick. His family runs a small fishing fleet here—the O'Connell Fishing Company. That might give us a natural in, especially if he can come back under the guise of helping with the family business."

"Excellent thinking. I'll speak to him about the possibility and keep you informed of our decision." Hayes's approval was clear in his tone. "Anything else I should know about the local situation?"

We hammered out a few more logistics—reporting schedules, communication protocols, and cover story details—before ending the call. I took a moment to send up a silent prayer of thanks that my gambit had worked and that my work, for once, was bringing me closer to what mattered instead of taking me away from it. Then, I slipped my phone back into my pocket and went in search of Gabi.

I found her finishing up with one of the EMTs, her professional demeanor intact despite the exhaustion I could see in the set of her shoulders. When she spotted me approaching, she wrapped up her conversation and walked over with a tired but genuine smile.

"Okay, *now* I can leave," she announced, pulling off the latex gloves she'd been wearing and tossing them in the nearest waste bin.

"Where to?" I asked, though I was pretty sure I already knew the answer.

"The clinic. That's where my car is, and by now they should have the debris cleared enough that I can get out of the parking lot." She rubbed her temples with her fingertips. "Plus, I want to check and make sure everything weathered the storm okay inside."

Despite the fact that I'd been up and moving almost constantly since before dawn, it felt good to move with unhurried purpose for the first time all day. The walk back to the clinic gave me precious time to gather my thoughts and plan what I wanted to say to her. The streets of Sutter's Ferry showed the aftermath of the hurricane—broken tree limbs, scattered debris, and the occasional piece of siding that had been torn loose from buildings. But the community was already rallying, with neighbors helping neighbors clear driveways and check on each other.

Her small sedan still sat beside the back door of the clinic, looking somewhat worse for wear. It had acquired a few more dings and scratches than it had possessed that morning, courtesy of flying debris, but all things considered, it had survived the hurricane remarkably well. The clinic itself was still boarded up tight, sheets of plywood covering every window like closed eyes. With all the medical staff deployed to the community center throughout the day, no one had been around to deal with reopening the building. Tomorrow, probably. It would be one more step on the long road back to normal. I had a feeling that both she and the rest of this tight-knit island community were going to need that sense of normalcy in the weeks to come.

Once inside, I helped Gabi check that everything was secure after the storm's passage. We moved through the building, testing equipment, checking for water damage, and wrestling mattresses back to their proper locations in the patient rooms. The familiar routine seemed to calm her, giving her tired mind something concrete and manageable to focus on.

As we worked together to maneuver the last mattress back into place, it occurred to me that with all the rush to get to Willa after her accident, I hadn't given Gabi the update I could about Mickey's break-in and what it meant for the clinic's safety.

"About Mickey," I said, settling the mattress on the bed frame and turning to face her. "You should know he was working alone. The break-in wasn't part of any larger operation targeting the clinic. He got himself in trouble with some dealers over in Manteo, owed them a significant amount of money, and thought stealing prescription medications would solve his problems fast."

Relief washed over her face like sunrise, and I watched her shoulders relax for the first time since I'd told her about the break-in. "So the clinic isn't in any ongoing danger? There's no organized effort to target our drug supplies?"

"No immediate threat, no. Your security protocols are solid, and this was just one desperate guy making bad choices." I rocked back on my heels, shoving my hands into my back pockets as I met her dark eyes. "But that leads me to something else I need to tell you. Something that's going to affect both of us."

Her eyebrows drew together, and I could see her preparing for bad news. "What is it?"

"I'm being assigned here to Hatterwick. Part of an ongoing federal task force operation that's going to require a long-term presence on the island." The words came out in a rush, and I watched her face for her reaction.

"I see." Her expression stayed neutral, giving me no clue what she was thinking.

Did she really see? Did she understand what this meant, or was she already building walls to protect herself?

She crossed her arms over her chest, and my stomach dropped. "For how long exactly?"

"Few months minimum, potentially longer. Depends on what intelligence gets uncovered while I'm here and how deep this smuggling operation goes." I stepped closer, close enough to catch the faint scent of her vanilla shampoo mixed with the antiseptic odor that clung to her scrubs. "Look, I won't pretend the job isn't what made this assignment possible. But Gabi, you're the reason I wanted it. You're the reason I volunteered for it."

Her expression softened, but she didn't uncross her arms or step toward me.

"I know I messed up before—catastrophically. Taking that Seattle position without even talking to you first, making that decision in isolation like your feelings didn't matter? That was the stupidest, most selfish thing I've ever done." The words tasted bitter, but they needed to be said. "I threw away the best thing in my life because I was too proud and too scared to admit I needed you more than I needed career advancement."

She listened intently, her dark eyes searching my face for signs of sincerity.

"Despite what happened between us last night, I'm not asking to pick up where we left off like nothing happened. I haven't earned that right, and I know it. But I'd like a chance to show you I've changed. That I understand now what I threw away and what really matters. That I'm willing to do the hard work to find the right balance between personal and professional responsibilities." I ran a hand through my hair, suddenly feeling every hour of sleep I'd missed. "Maybe we could start slow? Coffee sometime, when things settle down and you've had time to process all this?"

I held my breath, waiting for her answer, my heart hammering against my ribs so hard I was sure she could hear it.

The silence stretched between us for an eternity. Gabi's dark eyes searched my face with an intensity that stripped me bare, and I forced myself to stay still under her scrutiny. To let her take whatever time she needed to weigh my words against my past actions, to decide if I was worth the risk of trusting again.

Finally, after what seemed like hours but was probably only thirty seconds, she uncrossed her arms.

"You juggled everything today," she said slowly, thoughtfully. "In the middle of all the post-hurricane chaos and your federal investigation and securing crime scenes, you still made time for me. You took me to help my friend when she needed it. You put what mattered to me ahead of what was convenient for your case." A smile tugged at the corner of her mouth, small but genuine. "That means a lot to me, Daniel. More than you know."

My breath caught in my throat, and I took a half step

forward, drawn by that hint of warmth in her voice, by the hope I was afraid to let loose in my chest.

"So," she continued, and her smile grew wider, "I think we can do a lot better than coffee."

The words hit me like lightning, and that hope bloomed wild and desperate. But I forced myself to stay cautious, to make sure I understood what she was offering before I let myself believe it.

"Better than coffee?" Despite the mule kick of my heart against my ribs, I kept my voice neutral, not wanting to assume anything or push too hard too fast.

Her slow, devastating smile pulled me in like gravity, like coming home after years in exile. "Much better than coffee," she murmured, closing the last few inches of distance between us with deliberate, measured steps.

She flowed into my arms like she belonged there, like she'd never left, like the past months of separation and heartbreak had been nothing more than a bad dream. My hands curved around her waist, spanning the narrow space between her ribs and hips, and her fingers curled into the fabric of my shirt like she was anchoring herself to me.

Then her lips met mine, soft and warm and absolutely perfect, and the rest of the world disappeared.

She melted against me with a soft sigh, and I sank into the taste of her, into the flavor of forgiveness and possibility and everything I'd been missing since I'd made the worst decision of my life. I pulled her closer, needing to feel every inch of her pressed against me, savoring the way her hands slid up my chest to link behind my neck, the way she fit against me like we'd been designed for each other.

When we finally came up for air, both of us breathing hard, I rested my forehead against hers, closing my eyes and just breathing in this moment. The crushing weight that had been sitting on my chest since Seattle finally lifted, and my shoulders relaxed for the first time in months.

"I missed you," I whispered against her hair, my voice rough with emotion. "Every single day. Every single hour."

She hummed in contentment, her fingers playing with the hair at the nape of my neck. "I missed you too. Even when I was furious with you. Especially when I was furious with you."

"I deserved your fury. I deserved a lot worse than that, honestly."

"You did." She pulled back just enough to meet my eyes, her expression serious but not cold. "But you also earned this second chance today. With your actions, not just your words. Just don't mess it up, Daniel. I won't give you a third."

"Not a chance." I traced my thumb along the curve of her jaw, marveling at the softness of her skin. "I learned my lesson the hard way. No more making major life decisions without talking to you first. No more putting career ambition ahead of what really matters."

"Speaking of major life decisions..." She raised an eyebrow, a hint of mischief creeping into her expression. "Where exactly are you planning to stay during this extended assignment?"

"The firehouse, for now. Chief Thompson set up a cot in one of the back rooms, but it's definitely not a long-term solution." I gave her a hopeful look, not quite daring to ask directly but letting the question hang in the air between us. "You wouldn't happen to know of any apartments for rent on the island? Preferably something with a reasonable commute to a certain beautiful doctor's place?"

I HOPE you enjoyed your trip to Hatterwick Island! If this was your first visit, you should know that the series begins with a prequel novel, *Smoke on the Water*, that tells Caroline and Hoyt's story. If you're more interested in Willa and Sawyer and the events alluded to at the end here, check out their book *Won't Back Down.*

You can get an extra glimpse of Gabi and Daniel's happily ever after! Get the bonus epilogue straight to your inbox! Just sign up here: https://harperjacksonbooks.com/against-the-wind-be/

The series continues with Bree and Ford in *All Along The Watchtower*!

Ford Donoghue broke my heart a decade ago. And no matter how hard I tried, I was never really over it.

I perfected the art of ignoring him whenever he came home to Hatterwick Island—cold shoulders, polite smiles, and walls a mile high.

It worked.

Until the day his thirteen-year-old daughter walked into my bar, scared and looking for a father she's never met.

One phone call later, Ford's back in Hatterwick.

And so are all the feelings I swore I'd buried.

But this isn't about us.

At least, it wasn't supposed to be.

When a body washes up on the beach, the whole island goes on edge.

And when strange things start happening around Peyton, it's impossible not to wonder if her late mother's secrets are still casting shadows.

The more we dig, the more tangled the truth becomes.

And if we're wrong about where the danger's coming from, the girl who brought us back together might be the one who pays the price.

Turn the page for a sneak peek!

SNEAK PEEK ALL ALONG THE WATCHTOWER

FORD

Ford Donoghue broke my heart a decade ago. And no matter how hard I tried, I was never really over it.

I perfected the art of ignoring him whenever he came home to Hatterwick Island—cold shoulders, polite smiles, and walls a mile high.

It worked.

Until the day his thirteen-year-old daughter walked into my bar, scared and looking for a father she's never met.

One phone call later, Ford's back in Hatterwick.

And so are all the feelings I swore I'd buried.

But this isn't about us.

At least, it wasn't supposed to be.

When a body washes up on the beach, the whole island goes on edge.

And when strange things start happening around

Peyton, it's impossible not to wonder if her late mother's secrets are still casting shadows.

The more we dig, the more tangled the truth becomes.

And if we're wrong about where the danger's coming from, the girl who brought us back together might be the one who pays the price.

"Dude, it wasn't your fault."

Sawyer wouldn't stop pacing, looking like he was gonna puke. "How is it not my fault? If I hadn't helped her sneak out…" He raked his hands through his hair. "She almost died, Ford. If Willa had—God. Jace is never gonna forgive me."

"Bullshit." Rios wasn't having any of it. "Willa was gonna find a way to that party no matter what. If you hadn't brought her, hadn't noticed she was missing…" He didn't finish the thought. Didn't have to.

Yeah, Sawyer had helped Jace's little sister sneak past her helicopter parents to get to the beach party, but he'd also saved her life. He was the one who realized she was gone, spotted her in the water, and went in after her like some crazy action hero during the storm. Did CPR until she started breathing again. Got her help. She was alive because of him, even if she was stuck in the hospital on the mainland right now. Jace had gone with his parents, and we'd been waiting to hear something—anything—for hours.

Sawyer was still in his wet clothes from the party, looking like a half-drowned rat. Mom and Mimi had tried to get him to change, but he wouldn't listen. If Jace hadn't told us to keep an eye on him, Sawyer would probably still be out there on the beach, storm or no storm.

Nobody had any clue how Willa ended up in the water. She grew up here—she wasn't some tourist who didn't know better. She'd been swimming since before she could walk. Something about it felt wrong. Thank God Sawyer had spotted her at all. It had been a damned miracle he hadn't drowned trying to save her. Life would seriously suck without Sawyer Malone. He wasn't just my best friend—he was my brother. All the Wayward Sons were.

None of us had slept. My moms went up hours ago, but they kept checking in like we were little kids again. Sawyer wasn't gonna crash until we knew Willa was okay, so here we were, keeping watch with him. I tried not to think about what would happen if she wasn't okay.

The storm finally died down around sunrise. Still no text from Jace. He had to be just as wrecked as we were.

I could hang here with Sawyer as long as he needed, but we were gonna need fuel to keep our eyes open. I looked at Rios. "Coffee?"

"Hell yes. And maybe raid Mimi's cookie jar?"

"She'll kill you if she catches you eating cookies for breakfast."

The shadow of Rios's usual smartass grin appeared. "Please. I'm her favorite, and you know it."

"You wish." But before I could make it to the kitchen, someone pounded on the front door. We all froze.

"Who the hell?" Rios muttered.

"Maybe it's Jace." The hope in Sawyer's voice made my chest hurt.

But when I yanked open the door, it was Bree standing there looking like she hadn't slept either. She had that look she got when everything was going sideways—all pale and tense, arms wrapped around herself like she was holding something in.

"I know it's crazy early," she said, "but I saw the lights on. I'd have texted, but..."

"What's wrong?"

"Gwen's missing."

Gwen Busby was one of Willa's besties. She and Rios's younger sister, Gabi, were their own tight friend group. The three of them were a few classes under all of us, so we didn't exactly hang out, but we kept an eye on them. They'd absolutely been together last night at the party, before everything had gone to shit.

"What do you mean, missing?" Rios demanded.

"No one has seen her since the party last night. Her parents raised the alarm when she didn't come home. They're putting together an island-wide search. I figured y'all would want to be there."

Rios shook his head. "But that's impossible. I saw her myself when we were clearing out right before the storm hit."

"Chief Carson will want to hear about that, for sure. All I know is, she didn't make it home last night."

I scooped a hand through my hair. "Could she have gone home with somebody else?"

"Who?" Sawyer asked. "Willa's still in the hospital, and she didn't go home with Gabi."

"I mean... maybe a guy?" I suggested. "There was a lot of hooking up at that party."

"She's not that girl," Bree argued. "I mean, first time for everything, and it's not like I'm exactly an expert on normal teenage girl behavior since I spend all my time hanging out with you yahoos, but I don't see her willingly staying out all night with some guy."

She let the implication hang until we were all moving to grab our shoes.

My moms came downstairs, both in their bathrobes, eyes heavy from sleep.

Mom's eyes cleared when she spotted the four of us. "Is there news about Willa?"

"Not yet. Gwen Busby never made it home last night. They're organizing a search," I explained.

Mom and Mimi exchanged a look.

Mimi clutched the lapels of her robe together, her dark eyes full of worry. "We'll go dress."

Forty minutes later, we were spread out near Osprey Beach, where the party had been held last night. In the wake of the storm, there was no sign of the hundred or so teens who'd been here, except for the blackened pile of wood that was all that remained of the bonfire. Seaweed and driftwood were scattered all across the beach, along with the usual mess following a storm. If there'd ever been any footprints or other obvious signs to follow, they were definitely gone now.

An incident command tent had been set up at the edge of the boardwalk. The officer running things had organized all the searchers into a line to begin walking the area in a grid pattern. Hatterwick Island was only thirteen miles long and three miles across at its widest point. While it wasn't a big island, there were still plenty of places for someone to disappear, like the woods that occupied the center of the island going north. Maybe Gwen had tried to find shelter from the storm and injured herself. Sprained an ankle or something and hadn't been able to make it out.

"Gwen!" I shouted her name, my voice dying out in the heavy, humid air.

We made our way into the woods, continuing forward in our grid pattern. The morning ticked slowly by with her name becoming a chorus from all the searchers. I wondered again if she'd gone off with some guy. Had anybody been creeping on her? Was there some asshole out there who'd pressured her to do something she hadn't wanted to? I tried to think back to last night, to whether I'd seen anything. But the truth was, Gwen was someone at my periphery. Friend of a friend. I knew her, but she was younger. Only fifteen to our eighteen. She wasn't a direct part of our group, and all I'd been concerned with last night was enjoying myself and the start of the last summer I'd spend on the island with all the Wayward Sons before we split up in the fall.

Up ahead, someone bolted through the trees. "Gwen? Gwen! Where are you?"

I recognized that panicked voice as belonging to Miles Busby, Gwen's college-age older brother.

I picked up my pace and caught up with him. "Hey, man."

Miles whirled on me, his eyes almost feral with panic.

I lifted my hands in peace. "You okay? You need some water?"

"I need my sister."

"I get it. We're all looking. But maybe you should drink down some water. If you keel over from dehydration, you won't do her any good." I offered him some of my own water.

After a long hesitation, he took it, drinking down half the bottle. His eyes closed on a defeated sigh. "I'm her big brother. I was supposed to look out for her. And now she's..." His voice choked off.

"Hey, you don't know that. She might be fine."

But I could see he didn't believe that. And as the day progressed, and the search continued, with no word, no sign of her whatsoever, I was starting to get a really bad feeling that something terrible had happened to Gwen Busby.

Grab your copy of *All Along The Watchtower* today!

OTHER BOOKS BY HARPER JACKSON

Wayward Sons

- *Smoke on the Water: Hoyt and Caroline*
- *Won't Back Down: Sawyer and Willa*
- *Against the Wind: Daniel and Gabi*
- *All Along The Watchtower: Ford and Bree*
- *On the Other Side: Rios and Madden*
- *Carry On Wayward Son: Jace and Layla*—Coming August 2026

ABOUT THE AUTHOR

Harper Jackson has rescued her co-workers from a hostage situation, battled ninjas, and stopped international espionage—in her head anyway. Now that she's no longer busy devising ways to make staff meetings more entertaining, she's pouring that imagination into tales of breath-stealing, small-town romantic suspense. She believes that peach cobbler with ice cream is the best dessert ever and has a black belt in taekwondo to back it up. She lives in the Deep South with her husband and canine furbabies. Find out more about Harper and her books at https://harperjackson.com or explore the lighter side of her catalog as Kait Nolan at https://kaitnolan.com.